SORRY
FOR YOUR
LOSS

SORRY
FOR YOUR
LOSS

Joanne Levy

ORCA BOOK PUBLISHERS

Copyright © Joanne Levy 2021

Published in Canada and the United States in 2021 by Orca Book Publishers.
orcabook.com

All rights reserved. No part of this publication may be reproduced
or transmitted in any form or by any means, electronic or mechanical, including
photocopying, recording or by any information storage and retrieval system now
known or to be invented, without permission in writing from the publisher.

Library and Archives Canada Cataloguing in Publication
Title: Sorry for your loss / Joanne Levy.
Names: Levy, Joanne, author.
Identifiers: Canadiana (print) 20210105631 | Canadiana (ebook) 20210105844 |
ISBN 9781459827073 (softcover) | ISBN 9781459827080 (PDF) | ISBN 9781459827097 (EPUB)
Classification: LCC PS8623.E9592 S67 2021 | DDC jc813/.6—dc23

Library of Congress Control Number: 2020951477

Summary: In this novel for middle readers, twelve-year-old Evie
befriends a boy who is grieving the loss of both his parents.

Orca Book Publishers is committed to reducing the consumption of
nonrenewable resources in the making of our books. We make every
effort to use materials that support a sustainable future.

Orca Book Publishers gratefully acknowledges the support for its
publishing programs provided by the following agencies: the Government of Canada,
the Canada Council for the Arts and the Province of British Columbia through
the BC Arts Council and the Book Publishing Tax Credit.

Cover artwork by BIBIARTS/Creative Market,
Edgar Bibian / EyeEm/Getty Images, sbayram/Getty Images,
MarkGabrenya/Getty Images, T.SALAMATIK/Shutterstock.com and Sena Runa
Cover design by Rachel Page
Edited by Tanya Trafford
Author photo by Tania Garshowitz

Printed and bound in Canada.

24 23 22 21 • 1 2 3 4

For Dad.
For all the reasons you would expect, and a million more.

Last summer

"You should use crepe paper for that," said the boy sitting beside me.

It was only my second day at Camp Shalom, and we were doing crafts in the big lodge. We were supposed to be sailing, but it had been canceled because of thunderstorms.

The counselor had just given us an introduction to the art of paper quilling. She showed us how to coil strips of paper into different shapes. I was making a flower—one round coil for the center and a bunch of teardrop shapes for the petals.

Well, I was *trying* to make a flower—it just wasn't going so well.

I looked up at the kid who'd spoken to me. His friendly smile reached right up to his brown eyes. I liked him immediately. But I'd been so focused on getting the tiny rolls perfect that I hadn't actually heard what he'd said.

I blinked at him a couple of times. "Sorry, what?"

He glanced down at the red paper strip in my hands. It—and my fingers—were covered in glue. "You're making a flower, right?"

"Ha!" I said. "I'm surprised you could tell!"

He laughed. "Crepe paper would make it look more realistic. Thinner and more wavy and fluttery, you know? Like real petals on an actual flower."

I stared at him for a second. His shaggy brown hair was exactly the same color as his eyes. He shrugged. "Just saying."

"Huh." I considered the mangled mess pinched between my fingers. I tried to picture my daisy made with the thinner, crinkly crepe paper. The stuff that reminded me of birthday streamers. "Maybe you're right," I said. "I kind of like that idea. Thanks."

He flicked his bangs out of his eyes with a nod. "The texture makes it more interesting than regular flat paper."

"What are *you* making?" I asked, pointing my chin at the stack of colorful paper squares in front of him. They weren't cut into thin strips like the rest of us were using.

He smiled again. "I like folding—origami," he said. "I tried working with the strips last year, but they're too small." He held up his fingers and wiggled them. "My dad says I have big hands made for throwing footballs. Origami's more my jam."

To show me, he took one of the squares—a pink one—and folded it in half. And then he turned it and folded it again. His fingers moved so quickly I lost track of the steps. Over and over he folded the paper—this way, that way. Next thing I knew, he was handing me something that looked a lot like the hydrangeas Mom had in her garden, the ones I used to call "flower pom-poms."

If I hadn't just watched him make it, I'd never have believed that you could turn a sheet of paper into a beautiful flower.

"Whoa," I said, examining it more closely. So many tiny folds. "That's...whoa. This is really cool. Can you show me how to do it?"

He grinned at me, his sort of crooked teeth all on display. "I'm Sam, by the way."

I liked the way his eyes crinkled at the corners and smiled back.

"I'm Evie. Well, it's Evelyn, but you can call me Evie—that's what I like best. Some people, like teachers, and my parents when they're mad, call me Evelyn, but I prefer Evie. *Just* Evie," I said. And then, because I was worried I was being too bossy, I added, "Please and thank you."

"So let me get this straight. You're saying I should call you Evelyn?" the boy—Sam—replied. "That's what you're telling me?"

I laughed. "Exactly. What about you? Is your full name Samuel? Or is it Samson, like in the Torah?"

"It *is* Samson," he said, surprised. "But most people just assume it's Samuel, so good on you."

And just like that, our friendship began. All because of paper flowers. It sounds like a dad joke to say our friendship *bloomed*. But that's how it happened.

Unfortunately, later that summer I learned that, just like flowers, friendships can wither away.

That's when I decided I was done with having friends.

One

I am not obsessed with death.

But it's a bit hard to avoid thinking about death when your family owns a funeral home and everyone works there. Including me.

My part-time job at the Walman Memorial Chapel—my family's last name is Walman—includes cleaning and stocking the bathroom with paper towels and toilet paper. I am also in charge of making sure there are always plenty of tissues for the mourners. Dad calls me Purveyor of Paper Products. I call *him* His Royal Highness of Dad Jokes.

But right now I was thinking about a totally different kind of paper. I had just loaded up on craft supplies at my favorite stationery store.

"I can't wait to get started on my projects," I said to Suzanna, the owner, as she slid all my purchases into a bag. I bounced from one foot to the other. I was pretty excited about the vellum I had found. It was so delicate, almost see-through. I'd also gotten some heavy card stock with pretty deckled edges and some fancy handmade papyrus. I guess you could say I *am* obsessed with paper.

This was all because of Sam showing me how to quill last summer. I couldn't help but think how much he would have liked what I'd bought today. He'd especially liked the delicate papers like vellum, which was maybe why I'd bought it, even though it could be incredibly hard to quill with.

"I'm looking forward to seeing them when you're done," Suzanna said with a smile, handing me the bag. "You're getting so good."

I love sharing my quilling projects with Suzanna because she is always so enthusiastic. And she was right—I really was getting good. "Can you let me know when that foil comes in?" I asked. "I have an idea for—"

Just then the big church bells outside bonged, announcing that it was two o'clock.

Shoot! I was supposed to *be home* by two.

The bells hadn't even stopped bonging when I got a text from Mom: **Where r u!!??**

Uh-oh.

My parents had wanted to send me back to summer camp like usual. They are always so busy at the funeral home, and they worried that once school was out I'd be bored and get in the way. But I'd told them I didn't want to go this year. I had my reasons. One of them was Sam, though they don't know anything about that.

Anyway, I am happy to work at the funeral home and make some money for my paper and other stuff. Plus, I am actually interested in learning more about how our family business works.

The deal was, if I didn't go to camp, I had to do all my chores, put in my hours at the funeral home and never, ever complain about being bored. Oh, and I had to promise to be on time for everything. Mom is a real "stickler for punctuality," as she likes to remind us all the time.

I said a quick goodbye to Suzanna and raced out of the store.

So fast, in fact, that I nearly took out a couple of people coming in.

"Whoa, sorry!" I blurted. But then I saw who it was. Miri and Sasha. Great. I had been hoping I wouldn't have to see them until September.

I muttered an apology I really wasn't feeling and tried to get past them.

Nope. They blocked the doorway and just looked at me.

I pasted a smile on my face. "Oh hey. How's your summer going? Can you believe we're going into eighth grade? Unbelievable, right? I am—having a good summer, I mean—even though I'm not going to camp this year. I'm helping out at the—well, at home, I guess. What are you two doing? Having fun?"

Finally I had to stop to take a breath.

Miri and Sasha just kept staring.

"Sorry," I muttered, even as I felt my face grow hot. I clamped my lips shut.

Miri snorted and rolled her eyes. "She's awfully chatty for a corpse, isn't she, Sasha?"

Here we go.

"Right?" Sasha said. "I mean, I thought corpses were quiet. I didn't realize they talk *nonstop*."

Do I even need to say it? Miri and Sasha are *the worst*.

Sasha wasn't done, either. She laughed at her own clever comment and then leaned in close. She took a loud sniff of my ponytail. "And ugh, she sure *smells* like death. Disgusting. You sure you're not a zombie, *Evil*?"

After my speech in class about how I was going to be a funeral director when I grew up, the two of them had come up with all kinds of mean nicknames that I am now mostly used to. Sort of.

I'd washed my hair that very morning. With the shampoo I'd made my mom buy after the *last time* Sasha said I smelled like rotting corpses.

The shampoo is strawberry scented. A part of my brain drifted away and started wondering if dead people smell like strawberries. And if they do, how Sasha would know. I'd never gotten close enough to the actual dead people at the funeral home to sniff them, but the building didn't smell like strawberries. Or any other type of fruit.

I wanted to tell them both to shut up. Also that, like I'd told them a million times before, my job at the funeral home doesn't include getting close to dead people, so I *couldn't* smell like one. But for once I kept my mouth shut. It wouldn't matter. They just didn't care. No matter how hard I tried to show them that I was a normal girl whose family just happened to own a funeral home, they kept picking on me.

After my speech, I'd made Dad come to career day to talk about what it was like to be a funeral director and how important a job it was. After all, eventually everyone needs one. I'd thought that would make things better. But no, it got even worse. Way worse. Now everyone at school thinks my *whole family* is weird and obsessed with death.

When you go to a small private school like I do, *everyone* knows everything about you, even the kids in different grades. I'd asked my parents to transfer me from Beit Sefer to a public school with a ton of kids who don't know me. But they said I should try to stick it out for eighth grade. After that, if I was still unhappy, we could talk about my going to a public high school.

Until then I was stuck with being known as Chatty Corpse Girl, Morticia, Evil and whatever other humiliating names they could come up with.

"What'd you buy, Goth Girl?" Sasha asked as she and Miri shifted to block my way completely. She reached for the bag in my hands. "Black eyeliner?"

I pulled the bag away before she could get it. "This is a *stationery* store," I said. "They don't sell eyeliner." And it wasn't like I even wore makeup. Duh.

"I know that!" Sasha barked. "I'm here to pick out my *bat mitzvah* invitations. For my *bat mitzvah*." I guess she was emphasizing the words to make it sound like a very big deal. "That you won't be invited to, by the way," she added.

This was a lie. At our school, when someone has their bar or bat mitzvah, they have to invite the whole class. It's only, like, twelve people, but is a rule.

"Like I'd even want to go!" I said. I added a "Pffft!" for good measure.

All right, so maybe I did sort of want to go, but only to show her and everyone else that I was a good person who didn't hold grudges. I definitely wouldn't have any fun though. Or maybe I *would* have fun just to show her how much I didn't care that she and Miri were so mean to me.

"Whatever," Sasha said, adding a loud cluck of her tongue as she leaned toward me.

Miri moaned and rolled her eyes back. "Don't get too close, Sasha—she might try to eat your braaaaaaain."

It was a pretty lousy impression of a brain-eating zombie, if you ask me.

"Oh, yeah. Right," Sasha said, backing up dramatically.

I fought back tears as I pushed past the girls. Just because I didn't *want* any friends didn't mean I was immune to these girls being so horrible.

I got on my bike, looping my bag over the right handlebar, and pedaled toward home. The tears poured out of me, but I took some comfort in thinking about how when I grew up and became a funeral director like my parents, I wouldn't have to worry about my clients being mean to me.

Because they'd already be dead.

Two

After I got home and put my paper away, I hurried next door. I'd worked at the funeral home on Sundays and after school sometimes, but now that school's out, I am there pretty much every day. That's worked out great for my parents, since the assistant funeral director, Danielle, takes the summers off to travel with her husband and kids. They drive around the country in an RV, going from campground to campground.

Mom and Dad still have another staff member, Syd, but they had planned to hire a summer student too. Then I came up with the perfect plan to avoid going back to camp, and now I am their summer student.

When there isn't a funeral going on, my job is mainly to make sure everything's clean and check that we have enough supplies. When there *is* a funeral, I direct people coming into the chapel. My older brother, Nate, is in charge of traffic outside and then hands out kippahs to the men who need to cover their heads. I hand out the printed programs and packets of tissues.

It doesn't seem like much, but when nearly everyone around you is crying or is about to start crying, it's important to make sure everyone has enough tissues. Dad always says that people shouldn't have to worry about little details at times like these. It's our job to take care of those little details.

My first task on this day was restocking the fridge in the quiet room with bottles of water. There had been a funeral the day before, and it had been scorching hot outside. People must have been really thirsty, because the fridge was nearly empty and the recycle bin was filled with empties. I was kneeling on the carpet, humming to myself as I stacked the shelves, thinking about how I'd better get out the vacuum next. Even if the carpet doesn't *look* dirty, Mom says it always needs a daily going-over.

I startled when I heard a noise behind me. My mother was standing in the doorway, her arms crossed. She was wearing a charcoal-gray jacket and matching skirt with a crisp white blouse underneath. Her pretty burgundy-and-gray scarf was tied around her neck. Her hair and makeup were perfect.

I knew what that meant. A family was coming in to arrange a funeral. Dad sometimes meets with families, but usually it's Mom's job.

"What time are they coming?" I asked.

Mom glanced up at the old wooden clock on the wall. "Your dad just left for the hospital. The family will be here in about an hour and a half."

I nodded. "Okay, I'm just going to finish this and then I'll get out of here." When families come to arrange a service, I am supposed to stay out of the way. Even though I find all the details interesting, I know it's a really difficult time for the people who have lost a loved one. My parents have to gently guide them in making all kinds of decisions and sometimes explain some of the important Jewish rituals that need to be followed during a funeral.

"Actually, Evelyn," Mom said, sitting down on one of the sofas, "the family...well...honey, this is a tough one." She sighed and looked up at the picture hanging on the wall. It's a photo of a group of rabbis at the Western Wall in Israel, which my dad took when he traveled there as a teenager. I don't think Mom was actually looking at it though. She seemed a little spaced out.

Finally she spoke again. "The family was in a very bad car accident. Both of the parents were killed. But their son—their only child—well, he survived, thank God."

"Oh," I said, my shoulders slumping. "That's really sad."

My mom looked very upset. While she and Dad are always kind and respectful of the families that come to see them, most of the time they don't get emotional. After all, people dying is part of their jobs.

They are used to it. But sometimes it gets to them. Like now.

"It is." Mom nodded, her voice catching. "*Really* sad. The boy is your age, Evie. He was pretty banged up."

"Oh?" I said again, my heart thumping hard. I didn't like thinking about kids my age getting injured. Or sick either. But I pushed that thought away. "Is it really bad?"

"Pretty bad," she said. "But not life-threatening. Some severe bruising and broken bones, I think."

I shivered, and not because of the air-conditioning. Just because I was around death all the time too didn't mean I was okay with it. Losing *both* of your parents? The worst. I had to push that thought away. Some things were just too horrible to think about.

"Anyway, Evie…" Mom let out another sigh. "I was hoping…umm…I know it's a lot to ask."

"What can I do?"

She gave me a little smile. "I was hoping you'd say that. The deceased woman's brother is coming in to make the arrangements. The son—his name is Oren—will be with him. I was hoping you wouldn't mind spending some time with him while your father and I meet with his uncle."

Really? She wanted me to help meet with a family? Just the son, but still. My very first family meeting.

I nodded, trying not to smile because you're not supposed to be happy about talking to someone about their family members dying. But I couldn't help being a little excited on the inside. It felt like I'd just been promoted from cleaner and tissue girl to junior funeral director.

"Okay," I said, already thinking of what I would say to him. I could explain the funeral process and help him learn the special prayers, and give him the black ribbon he'd have to tear and put on his clothes and…my mind whirled. I didn't even realize Mom was still talking.

"…you can stay with him in here while we meet with his uncle in the office. If he has any questions or wants to be involved in any way, we'll honor that, of course," she said. "But I imagine he'll be more comfortable in here, where it's quiet. And with someone his own age." She gave me a smile. "And I bet you can answer just about any question he might have."

I smiled back at her. "That's true." I did know a lot about funerals. I might not be allowed to *do* stuff, but that didn't mean I couldn't prepare for the day when I would start working as a real funeral director. I couldn't wait to really help people and *do* something, not just sit back and watch. Yes, tissues were important, but I could do more. I wanted so badly to do more.

"Thank you, Evie," Mom said. "That will be really helpful."

"Of course," I said, closing up the little fridge and standing up. I brushed some dust off my shorts. "I'll do a quick vacuum first and then I'll go get changed."

Mom got up off the couch and sighed again. "I feel so terrible for this boy. One day all is well, and the next, his entire life is changed." She reached up and adjusted the picture, even though it wasn't crooked. "I'm sure he could use a friend more than anything right now."

"Okay," I said, because it was the answer Mom expected. But I had no intention of being this boy's friend. *Nope*. Never again.

What had happened to him was awful. Of course, I'd help him. Being a funeral director—even a junior one—meant I would always help out someone who was grieving. But that was it. No more.

Mom gave me one of her looks. "Evie, I know I don't need to remind you to be respectful, kind and on your best behavior, right?"

I rolled my eyes. "You mean like you just did?"

Mom smirked. "Right. And maybe..."

She paused for so long that I had to say, "Maybe *what*?"

"Er...well...maybe...don't talk his ear off?"

I lifted an eyebrow.

She lifted one of hers back at me.

"Fine," I said with a sigh, because okay, yes, in my family I am sort of known as a talker. A big talker. Like, a nonstop talker.

Out of nowhere Mom grabbed me by the shoulders and pulled me into a bear hug.

"Urk," I gurgled when she squeezed me really tight. "Mom!"

"Shush. Indulge your mother."

Another thing about being the daughter of funeral directors? You get used to a lot of random and spontaneous hugs.

Three

I was nervous. Not because this was my first time helping out with a family at the funeral home. Even though it was.

Okay, maybe that was part of it. A biggish part. But not all of it.

Mostly I was worried that I'd say something wrong. Yeah, I am a talker. And I sometimes get rambly, especially if I'm nervous. And then when I *realize* I'm rambling, I get *even more* nervous and then, well, you see where I'm going with this. Because here I am rambling. About rambling.

Anyway, there I sat in the funeral home office with my parents, waiting for Oren and his uncle to arrive.

"Evie!" Mom said. For the third time. Because I just couldn't seem to stop my leg from bouncing, making the chair squeak.

"Sorry!" I muttered, hooking my foot around the chair leg to keep it still.

With clammy hands, I smoothed my dark gray skirt. I was also wearing a black top and matching cardigan, my standard funeral outfit. Respectful, plus it would keep me warm in the very air-conditioned funeral home. My black shoes were starting to pinch my toes.

Finally the front door opened with a soft *whoosh*.

Mom and Dad exchanged a nod as they got up from their seats. I stood up too. My left shoe was definitely getting tight.

Dad came around the desk and gave me an encouraging smile as he put one hand on my shoulder and guided me toward the lobby. Not that he needed to, but it was nice. Somehow he always seems to know when people need encouragement or comforting—that's probably what makes him such a good funeral director.

I noticed the tall man standing there first. He was probably younger than Dad, but in some ways he looked older. There were dark, puffy bags under his red-rimmed eyes, and it looked like he hadn't shaved. His shoulders sagged and his clothes were rumpled, like he'd slept in them. Maybe he had.

He didn't just look old, he looked exhausted and grief-stricken. I don't like seeing people like that—looking their worst. Even after attending as many funerals as I have (twenty-four), it still makes me sad.

Beside him stood the boy, who I already knew was Oren Katzman. He was about my height, but that was pretty much all I could tell about him. I couldn't see his eyes because his head was bowed, his longish dark hair falling forward and covering his face.

"Mr. Silver," Dad said, taking his hand off my shoulder and extending it toward the man. "I'm so sorry for your loss." Mr. Silver nodded, and Dad turned to Oren. "And my deepest condolences to you as well, Oren." He didn't offer his hand to him, probably because Oren's right arm was in a sling. I noticed that the cast, which covered most of his hand and went right up to his elbow, was impossibly clean and white. Brand-new.

The boy nodded.

"Oren," Mom said gently. "This is our daughter, Evelyn. She'll take you to the quiet room while we work out the arrangements with your uncle."

I held my breath. Oren finally lifted his head. It was then that I saw he had two black eyes and a jagged line of stitches along his bruised right cheek.

I swallowed a gasp as my stomach lurched. Not because his injuries were gross, but because they made everything feel very real. This boy had been in a horrible car wreck. This boy had lost both of his parents. This wasn't a movie. This was real life.

Oren didn't look at me but instead fixed his eyes on his uncle.

"Oh," Mr. Silver said. "Can you tell me where your bathroom is, please?"

Dad pointed down the hall. "Second door on the right."

Without a word Oren turned and walked toward the men's room. For some reason, we all watched him go. He pushed open the door and then disappeared.

Mr. Silver sighed. "He hasn't said a word since the accident."

"Oh?" Dad said.

Mr. Silver shook his head. "They checked him out—it's nothing physical. And what little sleep he did get last night—well, he had nightmares." He glanced at me before adding, "He did...vocalize then, so it's not that he *can't* speak."

I wondered if "vocalize" really meant scream, but it wouldn't be right to ask.

"Give him time," Mom said. "He's still in shock. It will take a while for him to sort out his feelings."

"He's a good kid," Mr. Silver said, nodding. "I'm his guardian now. It's what my sister wanted, but...of course we never thought...this has...it's all...it's been... wow." He took a long breath. "My sister is...*was*..." His face crumpled, and he began to sob. Like, not just a few tears, but I mean *really* sob.

This happens a lot at the funeral home. It's why we buy tissues by the case.

I had to look away. Thinking about cases of tissues seemed ridiculous when people who had been utterly devastated were standing right in front of you.

Out of the corner of my eye, I saw Mom put an arm around Mr. Silver. She muttered comforting things to him as she guided him toward the office.

"We'll give them a minute," Dad said. "You okay?"

It took me a second to realize he was talking to me. It was then that I noticed my own eyes had filled with tears. "Yes," I squeaked out before I cleared my throat. "It's so sad. How do you do this every day, Dad? Isn't it hard?"

He sighed. "It *is* hard," he said. "Especially when it's about kids and people being taken from us far too soon. While you learn to *deal* with grief—recognizing it and accepting it—no matter how many years you do this job, you are never immune. But being there for people in their time of need is an honor. It's a mitzvah to help families this way."

I'd heard him say that before about the mitzvah—a good deed—but it was weirdly comforting to know that sometimes it was hard for him too.

"Still want to work here when you grow up?"

It was like he'd been reading my mind. I nodded. "I think so."

Dad reached out and tucked a piece of my hair behind my ear. "You've got lots of time to decide for sure," he said gently. "We don't *expect* you to join the family business, Evie."

But I already had decided. Dad didn't know the big reason why, but I'd made up my mind almost a year ago.

"Like, right now your brother says he wants to get into computers or game design, and that's fine," Dad continued. "But that doesn't mean he won't change his mind next year. Your mom and I will support you both 100 percent in whatever career path you choose. We do appreciate you helping us out so much though."

In addition to pitching in on funeral days, Nate also maintains the chapel's website. He's only fourteen, but has already started talking about studying computer science. Sounds like a lot of big talk to me. Now if there were a job where you could sit on the couch eating chips and playing video games, he definitely would have a rewarding career ahead of him.

"But if you *do* decide you want a career in the industry," Dad continued, "you'd be very good at it." He smiled again, a little wider this time. "And I'm not just saying that because I'm your father."

He looked down the hall. "Why don't you go wait for Oren and take him straight into the quiet room? Let me know if you need anything."

I nodded and began walking away.

"Oh, and Evie?"

"Yeah?"

"Just…you know…just don't—" He winced.

"Talk his ear off," I said. "I know, Dad, I know."

I didn't have to wait long before Oren came out of the bathroom. He stopped abruptly in the doorway when he saw me standing there. The swinging door bumped into his butt.

"Your uncle is meeting with my parents in the office," I said, not mentioning the meltdown. "We can go to the quiet room." I pointed toward the back of the building. "That's where you'll be before the funeral, while people are coming in. That way you don't have to greet anyone."

Oren swallowed hard and then just stared at me. I replayed what I'd just said inside my head.

Duh, Evie! I could have smacked myself. *Why did you bring up the funeral?*

But the truth was, even though Oren probably didn't want to hear about it, the funeral had to happen very soon, whether he was ready or not.

Jewish people have funerals as soon as possible—sometimes even the next day—for a few reasons. The biggest one is to honor the dead. Some people say—the neshama—the soul—hangs around until the body is properly laid to rest.

I once asked Dad if that means there are ghosts hanging out in the funeral chapel all the time. He said he didn't really believe in ghosts, but that it was tradition to put bodies to rest quickly. For one thing, it helped the mourners begin to work through their grief. That seemed like a very good reason.

I couldn't say any of this to Oren though.

"I'm sorry," I said, fighting embarrassed tears. "Let's just…we'll go sit down. Okay?"

He looked toward the office again. I wasn't sure, but I thought I heard something that sounded like a sob.

Oren must have heard it too, because he turned back to me and nodded.

I led him down the hall to the quiet room. I flicked the light switch and gestured for him to enter. The room was decorated with blue walls and soft lighting to be calming and serene—almost like a living room. When Oren sat at the end of one of the sofas, I pointed at the small fridge. "Do you want some water?"

He shook his head.

"Right, okay, well, there's a bathroom in here too, if you need it," I said, pointing at a door on the other side of the room. "Which obviously you don't, since you just used the one down the hall. Please, make yourself comfortable."

Ugh, Evie! Stop talking! How could you be comfortable when your world had just been ripped apart? Not to mention what had happened to his body. It was hard not to stare at his injuries and wonder about them. Mom had said broken bones. I wondered what else besides his arm and his face was injured.

I took a seat at the other end of the couch. I was definitely going to have to figure out better things to say to families if I was going to have any hope of becoming a funeral director.

For the longest time, the only sound in the blue room was the *tick-tick-tick* of the clock on the far wall. I had to say *something*.

"I'm sorry I mentioned the funeral before," I said,

trying to remember the things I'd heard my parents say. "This is a very difficult time for you, I know. I mean, I obviously *don't* know because I haven't lost my parents, but I…um…I'm…my deepest condolences."

Oren looked down toward his lap and shrugged.

"You can talk to me about it if you want," I said. "I'm a good listener."

He didn't nod or even look at me.

"I'm…well, I'm not an official funeral director yet, but I will be someday. I know all about grief and can help you." His silence was starting to make me nervous again. "So yeah, you can talk to me. About how you're feeling. Or, you know, if you have any questions about anything. I know most of what goes on in the building. And like I said, grief is sort of my thing."

Still nothing.

"Or you could, you know, write stuff down. If you don't want to actually talk. Want me to get a pen and paper?"

He finally looked at me. It was not a friendly look. He narrowed his eyes and shook his head. At least now I could *see* his eyes. They were greenish brown—hazel, I guess. The bruises and cuts around them stood out more than the color of his irises though.

I realized he was still staring at me. It was getting so awkward. We both dropped our eyes.

We sat, heads hanging down, on either end of the sofa for a long time while the clock ticked. And ticked. And ticked some more. Like it was counting down to eternity.

I suddenly felt like ripping the clock off the wall and tossing it out the back door like a Frisbee.

"Anyway," I said breaking the extremely uncomfortable silence. "You can call me Evie. I know my mother introduced me as Evelyn, and that *is* my name, but I prefer to be called Evie. Not *Evil*, as some kids at school like to call me. But they're mostly jerks and—"

He did look up at me then and lifted an eyebrow.

My face got hot. "I mean, if you were going to say my name at all. Which, obviously, you're not."

Stop rambling, Evie!

I waited for him to laugh or do something.

Nothing.

How the heck was I supposed to do this?

"Anyway," I said, after what felt like another really long time and when I just couldn't stand the silence any longer, "my mom asked me to hang out with you in case you had any questions. So do you? Have any questions, I mean?"

Oren shook his head.

This was not going well. How could you have a conversation with someone who didn't *say* anything? *Please, please, please just say something!*

Maybe telling him what to expect would help.

"Do you want me to go through what will happen at the funeral?"

This time Oren didn't shake his head, but he did exhale loudly through his nose.

Finally! He was going to speak! I held my breath. I wondered what his first words would be. Probably my name. Or a thank-you for being so supportive.

But instead of saying anything, Oren got up from the sofa and, without even a glance back at me, strode across the room.

He opened the door to the bathroom and then closed it behind him. I heard the lock turn with a loud *kerchunk*.

I guessed that meant he didn't have any questions.

Four

After several minutes I got up to listen at the bathroom door. Not so close that if Oren opened it, he'd assume I was eavesdropping, but near enough that I would be able to hear water running.

I heard nothing.

Oren wasn't actually *using* the bathroom. I didn't hear crying either, which was a good thing.

The bad thing? He was hiding from me. He probably wasn't coming out. Maybe ever.

Well done on your first family meeting, Evie. Could it have gone any worse?

I took a few breaths, willing myself not to cry, trying not to dwell on the fact that Oren must have thought I was babbling dork who couldn't stop talking. What was I supposed to do now?

My first instinct was to apologize through the door, but I'd already made him run away with my rambling, so *more* talking probably wasn't going to help. I'd been

warned not to talk his ear off—by *both* of my parents—
and that's exactly what I'd done.

How was I supposed to explain his being locked in the
bathroom to his uncle? To my parents?

Sigh. The truth, I guess.

I suddenly wanted to run away and hide too. But I
couldn't let Oren come out of the bathroom and think
he'd been abandoned.

I gently tapped on the door. "Um, hi, Oren…uh…
I'm going to go check on things. You just make yourself
comfortable and don't worry about anything, okay?"

I listened for a moment in case he wanted to respond
or come out.

Nope.

I hurried out of the room and down the hall toward the
office. At the door I could hear that my parents had gotten
down to business with Mr. Silver. My mother was talking
about limousines to take the family to the cemetery.

I peeked in through the office window. The three
of them were sitting at the table, paperwork spread
everywhere.

Thankful that Mr. Silver had his back to me, I did a little
wave to try to catch my dad's eye. It worked. His eyebrows
went up—he was asking me if everything was okay.

I shook my head. No, everything was most definitely
not okay.

He made his excuses and came out. "Evie?" he said,
softly closing the office door behind him.

That's when I burst into tears.

Of course, Dad is very experienced with weeping people. He put his arm around me and led me away from the office and into the chapel. "Evie? What happened?" he asked quietly as soon as we were inside. "Where's Oren?"

"Locked in the bathroom," I said, pointing in the direction of the quiet room.

I'd been prepared for Oren to be teary, so I had a packet of tissues in my pocket. I tugged two squares out and shoved them against my eyes before trying to explain.

"Remember how you said I'd be a good funeral director?"

"Yes," Dad said.

"Yeah, well, you were wroooooooooooong." That last word got stretched out because I was crying again.

"I don't think so," Dad said as he pulled me into a hug.

I worried about slobbering all over his clean white shirt, but I couldn't help it. After I calmed down, I pulled out of his arms and mopped up the rest of my tears.

"Tell me what happened," he said, tugging me over to a pew, where we both sat down.

Once I was done explaining, I took a few deep breaths and crumpled the damp tissues in my fists.

"Grief is a difficult thing," Dad said. "And losing a parent—let alone *two*—is life-changing at any age. But for someone so young, well, I can't imagine how awful it must be."

"And I just made it worse," I said.

Dad smiled sadly. "You may not have helped, but I doubt you made it worse. Look, Oren isn't in a place right now where *anyone* can say anything that will help. He needs to work through his grief, and all we can do is be there for whatever he needs. Even if what he needs is space and time to sort it out himself."

It made sense, but I still felt like I'd messed up. "And not some random girl who will talk his ear off."

Dad nodded and sighed. "I'm sorry to say you're probably right there, Evie. But you have to remember this isn't about you. Part of being a good funeral director— and even a good *friend*—is knowing that someone may not want to be consoled. They may not welcome your words of support, and you need to respect that. Someone else's grief is not for you to solve. Let Oren grieve in his own way."

I had wanted to help so badly. I thought about how hard I had tried to get him to talk. How I'd kept thinking how hard it was for *me*.

"Tell you what," Dad said. "Why don't you head home and get started on the salad for dinner. I'll go see about Oren. We're just about done with his uncle anyway."

"All right," I said, disappointed. I was already a giant failure in my role as a junior funeral director.

"Evie," Dad said, his hand landing on my shoulder before I could turn away. "Don't forget that dealing with grieving families is the hardest part of this job. You already have a take-charge attitude and good instincts—these are great qualities for a funeral director, and they can be hard to teach. But what you *can* learn is that everyone is different. Sometimes your take-charge attitude can get ahead of those good instincts. Learning how to read people and what they might need is part of the job too. That will come with time."

I didn't really believe him about the instincts thing, but I was glad to hear that at least some things can be learned. "When's the funeral?"

"Tomorrow," Dad said. "If Nate's home, let him know, okay? We'll need him to update the website as soon as we confirm the time with the rabbi."

"Sure."

"And of course, we'll need your help too," Dad said sadly. "We are expecting a fairly large crowd."

At least handing out tissues was something I couldn't screw up.

Five

Later that night I sat at the dining-room table with my giant craft box, working on my latest paper quilling project.

After I'd returned from camp last year, I'd used all my birthday money to buy a quilling starter kit. At first I'd made little things—flowers, hearts and simple random shapes. But now I was attempting more challenging things. Not just individual shapes, but incorporating those shapes into entire scenes.

The one I was working on now was a meadow filled with flowers and grass. All made from tiny strips of paper. And glue. Lots of glue.

I'd been working on it for nearly a week, and it was really starting to come together. It still needed a few things though, like a sun and some clouds. Maybe a few birds or butterflies.

But tonight I was having trouble concentrating.

"What's wrong, Evie?" my mom said, startling me. I hadn't even realized she was in the room.

"Huh?" I blinked up at her.

She sat down in the chair across from me. "Look at you!" She laughed. "You're covered in glue! It's even on your face—please don't get any on the chairs."

"Sorry." She was right. I was making a huge mess.

"So tell me what's going on with you."

"Nothing," I said.

"Evie," she said. "I know you. And I know when something's up. The two giant sighs you've let out in the last two minutes were a big clue too."

Weird. I hadn't even realized I'd sighed. I looked down at my fingers covered in glue. I could feel a tight patch of it drying on my cheek.

With a third sigh, I carefully closed the lid of the glue bottle. I thought about what I could say to my mom as I wiped my sticky hands on a paper towel. But I wasn't even sure what I was thinking.

"I..." Sigh number four. "I...can't stop thinking about him. Oren, I mean." I barely got his name out before I started to cry. Not just a few tears either. I dropped my head and really started to bawl.

Mom came around the table and crouched down beside me. "Honey, I'm so sorry," she said, looking up at me. I turned a bit as she put her hands on my arms. "I didn't realize that meeting him had affected you so much. It's such a horrible thing that happened to him. Do you want to talk about it?"

I nodded and then shook my head. I had a jumble of

feelings inside me, crashing together and mixing up—I wasn't sure they would make sense even if I tried to explain them.

She paused for a moment before she spoke again. "I'm sorry, Evie. I know it must be hard for you and Nate not to think about what could happen if…you know… considering what we do." It was her turn to sigh. "But… that accident that Oren was in? Things like that are very rare. Still, I understand how scary it must be for you."

I shrugged. "I try not to think about it, but…"

"I know," she said, tears in *her* eyes now. "I think your dad felt the same way, growing up with his parents running the business. He, just like you and Nate, was exposed to death much more than other kids. I think it made him more serious. Definitely a little risk-averse." She smiled even as she swiped at a tear with her thumb. "But you know that you can always talk to him or me about anything, right?"

"Yeah, I know." I sniffled. "It's not just that though. I mean, it kinda is, but it's more about Oren. I messed it all up. I made him—" I tried to take a deep breath and it turned into a weird sobbing hiccup "—even sadder."

"You didn't, Evie." Mom's hands slid down my arms to my hands, and she gave them a reassuring squeeze. "You were doing your best to help in a very difficult situation. To be honest, if your Dad and I had known more about what kind of state he was in psychologically, we probably wouldn't have asked you to help. I'm sorry for putting you in the middle of that."

"It's okay." I looked up at her. "I *wanted* to help. I just…" Would I *ever* get this stuff right?

"You *did not* mess up, Evie," she said almost sternly as she stared directly into my eyes. "Okay?"

I shrugged. I didn't believe her, but I didn't feel like arguing.

She gave me a final squeeze before she stood up. "Your father and I have to go next door now to do the taharas for Oren's parents. Nate is up in his room if you need anything."

She gave me a kiss on the top of my head before she left the room.

I suddenly wished they didn't have to go to work. Maybe if they didn't have to, Mom would sit and help me like she sometimes did—using my paper cutter to make strips for me while I twirled and arranged them into shapes. We could talk more about Oren and what it meant for him now that his parents were gone. Or maybe I could talk to my dad about what it was like for him growing up in this same house, watching his parents go to work in the funeral home right next door. Was it the same for him as it was for me?

But their jobs were important. Way more important than cutting up paper for crafts. And they couldn't wait. They were on call all the time whether they liked it or not.

Since the funeral was scheduled for the next day, Mom and Dad had to go help the chevra kadisha—the people who perform the special rituals to prepare the bodies for burial. Mom would help the group that prepared Oren's mother, and Dad would help prepare Oren's father.

I'd never seen a tahara done, but I knew what it was. And it was the part of working at the funeral home that I was dreading most. Can you blame me?

I didn't dread it because I was worried about zombies or ghosts. Or because I thought that death was contagious (my parents were proof that it wasn't) or that I'd start to *smell* like death the way the jerks at school said. It was mostly because performing a tahara meant you had to touch a dead person. Not just touch them, but wash them and dress them too. Even cleaning their nails was part of it. Pretty intense.

Dad says it's the ultimate mitzvah you can do for someone, because they can't thank you or ever return the favor. But it still sounds terrifying.

I guess that's why I'm not allowed to help with that until I am older.

And why I am in charge of tissues.

But as I sat there fiddling with my scissors and paper strips, giving out tissues didn't feel like enough. I thought about Oren and what he was going through. In an instant he had lost his entire family. How do you even start to recover from that?

I wanted to do more. And I needed him to know I was sorry for messing up earlier. And I wanted him to know how very sorry I was for his loss.

But how? I didn't want to make a fool of myself by talking his ear off (again).

I looked down at the little paper daisy in front of me. Blue on the outside, yellow in the middle, green for leaves and a stem.

Dad came into the room. "Looks great, Evie," he said. "It's really turning into a piece of art!"

"Thanks," I said, glancing up at him. He had a stack of papers in his hands. "What's all that?"

"I just printed out all the programs for tomorrow's funeral." He frowned. "I've never done a double funeral before. It makes sense, and I guess it will be easier on Oren in the long run, but..." He sighed and shook his head.

"Can I see?" I asked.

He handed me the top page. It looked like most of the programs I'd seen for previous funerals except that it had two people's names on it instead of one. The English and Hebrew names of Oren's parents, along with their birth dates and the date they died, also in English and Hebrew. The information about the funeral service and the location of the reception at the shiva house were there too, but only in English.

I glanced at my pile of colored papers and got an idea. Maybe there *was* something I could do for Oren.

"Can I keep this one?"

Dad tilted his head. "Sure. What are you going to do with it?"

"I don't know exactly," I said, even as I reached for my scissors.

Six

The service was set for 1:00 p.m. That meant I had the whole morning to make sure the chapel, quiet room and lobby were in tip-top shape. The pews were dusted and polished, the floors had been vacuumed. There was plenty of toilet paper and paper towels in the bathroom, and the tissues were stacked neatly on the table by the chapel doors.

Dad had just wheeled the two trolleys carrying the caskets to the front of the chapel, arranging them so everyone attending would be able to see them.

I was very aware that there were now two dead people in the room. I tried to put that knowledge out of my head. It helped that the lids of the caskets were closed. Mom had told me that other funeral homes sometimes have services with open caskets, so you can actually see the dead person. That never happens here, something I'm really thankful for.

Nate was out in the parking lot, setting up pylons with Syd, so I neatly arranged kippahs in the box at the chapel doors and straightened the pile of tissue packages. Then I vacuumed the lobby. For a second time.

When it was time for lunch, I grabbed a package of tissues from the top of the pile and jogged across the parking lot to the house. Mom was in the kitchen, making sandwiches.

As we ate, we talked about our upcoming camping trip. We were heading out in three weeks. We weren't doing the RV thing like Danielle and her family though. We would be camping old-school in a tent and cooking over a campfire. I'd never been camping before, so I was pretty excited.

Dad was looking forward to being away from screens and electronics for more than just Shabbat. Even though he loves his job, I could tell he was looking forward to some time away from the chapel too.

Nate had been grumbling about it for weeks. He was not looking forward to being away from screens and electronics.

After lunch I washed up, brushed my hair and changed into my funeral outfit. I grabbed the quilling project I'd worked on the night before. It was a stem with two flowers on it—one for each of Oren's parents. I'd used strips with their names on them, carefully cut from the program, to make the stems. Hebrew on one side, English on the other. The flowers were made of colored paper, and I'd left them plain except for the centers, where I'd written Oren's name with a fine-tip marker.

As I looked at them now, I suddenly felt silly. Would Oren even like them? His parents had just died. Even though these were the best ones I'd ever done, why would he care about fake paper flowers?

I almost threw them out. But then I decided what the heck. I taped them onto the back of the packet of tissues—they fit perfectly—and tucked the whole thing into my skirt pocket, being careful not to crush it.

"Evie, *please*," Mom scolded. Again.

"Sorry!" I curled my foot around the leg of the squeaky chair to keep my leg from bouncing. But it was either that or start rambling again.

I'd been to lots of funerals and I'd never been very nervous. But today I wasn't just nervous—I was *really* nervous. My heart raced, my stomach was filled with butterflies, and my hands were sweaty.

Mom, Dad and I were in the office, waiting for the family to arrive. A limousine was bringing them here early so they could be settled into the quiet room before the other people arrived.

At the sound of a car approaching, I followed Dad's gaze out the window. Nate was directing the limousine into the family spot by the big back doors, beside the two hearses.

"They're here," Dad announced unnecessarily.

We all stood. I was about to go out into the lobby when Dad said, "Evie…"

I knew exactly what he was going to say. I rolled my eyes. "Don't worry. I won't talk his ear off. I learned my lesson."

The three of us headed for the lobby. I ran the tips of my fingers over the paper flowers in my pocket, still not 100 percent sure I should give it to Oren. I mean, I wanted to. Sort of. But not if he'd think it was weird.

Oren and his uncle came through the door. They were both wearing black suits and ties and shiny black shoes. Oren's suit jacket was only draped over his right shoulder because his arm was in the sling. His face still looked awful—less puffy, but the colors of the bruises were brighter somehow. It had only been a day since I'd seen him. Barely any time to heal his body. Definitely not his heart.

Dad stepped forward and greeted Mr. Silver solemnly, then briefly placed a hand on Oren's left shoulder.

Behind them was an older couple, hunched over and holding each other up. Their faces were damp, and they looked overwhelmed with grief. Oren's grandparents, I guessed. I wondered briefly if they were his mom's parents or his dad's.

I took a breath to steady myself. I was determined not to cry. When I looked at my mom, I could see that her eyes were a bit glassy. But her emotions didn't stop her from doing her job, and I thought that was pretty amazing. She reached out to the older couple and murmured some comforting words. I was pretty sure I was going to get a lot of hugs from her and Dad later.

Continuing to speak in hushed voices, my parents began to lead everyone to the quiet room.

It's now or never, Evie. I decided on never. But just as I was about to turn away, Oren looked up. His hazel eyes looked right into mine.

It had to be a sign. I pulled the packet from my pocket and took the two steps over to him. "Sorry for your loss," I said. I'd said these words a million times before, the only thing you can say when you don't know what to say. But I'd never meant them so much as right now.

He didn't nod. Or smile. Or do anything but stare.

I wanted to fidget. The words started to bubble up. But I remembered the previous day's disaster and bit my lip, determined to keep my mouth shut. I held out the packet. "This is for you."

His eyes dropped to my outstretched hand. Without even looking at it, he took the packet and shoved it into his pocket. Then turned and walked toward the quiet room.

Seven

Dad had been right when he said it would be a large crowd.

After he and Mom had settled the family in the quiet room, Dad went outside to help Syd direct cars. They were starting to pour into the lot.

The cars all had to be parked in the right order, so that after the service the hearses and the limousine had a clear path out of the parking lot, leading the procession to the cemetery. Dad and Syd handed out the special funeral signs for people to put on their cars, as well as flyers with directions to the cemetery for anyone from out of town.

I took my position to the right of the entrance at the rear of chapel. Nate was on the left. We greeted people solemnly and handed out the tissues and kippahs. The pews began to fill up from the back, the mourners chatting in hushed tones as they waited for the service to begin.

I wasn't *trying* to eavesdrop, but more than once I overhead the phrases "such a shame," "gone too soon" and, more than anything else, "that poor boy."

Of course, they were talking about Oren.

"...couldn't his grandparents take him?" I heard as a couple of ladies approached. My ears perked up.

"One set's here, but neither of them is in good health, and they are in a care home. The mother's parents and another brother live in Israel. I'm sure that Jared will do fine, although it will be a big adjustment for them both."

I guessed that Jared was Mr. Silver—Oren's uncle.

"Is he at least dating anyone? That boy needs a mother."

"He took out the Feinberg girl a few—"

"Excuse me?"

Uh-oh. I had totally zoned out. One of the ladies was glaring at me. "I'm sorry!" I mumbled, handing her some tissues. "Uh...and for your loss!" I added. She tutted at me and proceeded into the chapel. My face was burning. I concentrated hard on my duties after that, blocking out all the distracting conversations, until it was time for the service to begin.

The chapel filled quickly—nearly every pew held people squished tightly together, and a few even stood at the back. At exactly one o'clock the rabbi entered the chapel from a side door and stepped up onto the raised platform behind the podium. The stragglers rushed in, and the crowd quickly hushed.

Oren's uncle, his grandparents and then Oren came

out of that same door and sat down in the front pew. The whole room was silent except for the occasional rustling of clothing, sniffling, and crinkling of tissue wrappers.

Most times I like attending the services. I get to learn about the people who died and hear the nice things others say about them. I don't know—it just feels good somehow. Sometimes people even say funny things that make everyone laugh through their tears. I've always thought that the person who had died—if they were still hanging around to listen—would like that.

But when I saw Oren's face as he came into the chapel and paused briefly in front of the two caskets, I knew this wouldn't be one of those times.

Nate stayed out in the lobby to attend to any late-comers. I closed the chapel doors and sat down in the last row at the back. Mom and Dad were already in their reserved spots by the side door.

The rabbi looked out at the crowd. His gaze drew us all in.

He began with a prayer in Hebrew. His deep voice resonated all the way back to me. He then switched to English and thanked everyone for coming.

His talk was full of really nice details about Mr. and Mrs. Katzman—Oren's parents. How they had lived lives filled with love and commitment, to each other, to their son and to their community.

It was nice learning more about these people I would never meet, even though by the time the rabbi was finished, every single person was crying—even me. I couldn't see Oren way up at the front but wondered what he was thinking. No matter how many nice things were said about his parents, nothing could bring them back.

Mr. Silver stepped up to the podium. He thanked everyone for coming and then told a funny story about his little sister at his bar mitzvah. She'd gone missing, and they had looked for her everywhere. They were about to call the police when they found her hiding under one of the tables. Their mother had forbidden her to touch anything from the dessert table, so she had grabbed a tray of cupcakes and was under the table, licking the icing off every one. That was Mindy, he said, defiant and headstrong. No one could ever tell her what to do.

He told the story with such love and laughter, but as soon as he was done, he broke. He started crying so hard he couldn't finish his speech. The rabbi stepped forward and gently guided him back to his seat.

One of Mr. Katzman's friends came up and talked about the couple for a bit. His eyes were focused on the front row, like he was speaking directly to Oren about how wonderful his parents were.

I wondered if Oren heard any of it. I hoped he would be able to remember some of it later.

A few more speeches, and then it was over. I glanced at my dad and saw him nod at one of the men in the second row, the cue for the pallbearers to come up to the front. They would carry the caskets out to the hearses that had been backed up to the big side doors on the far side of the chapel.

We own just one hearse—Dad's old retro one that he named Ecto after the one from the *Ghostbusters* movie. For today's service, one of the other funeral homes in town had loaned us a hearse and driver.

The family stood up. The pallbearers lifted the caskets by their wooden handles and made their way to the doors. Mr. Silver put an arm around Oren and pulled him close. I couldn't really see their faces. I wanted to, though I didn't know why. I already knew they were sad.

Once the caskets were loaded into the backs of the hearses, the drivers closed the swinging rear doors. The *kerchunk, kerchunk* seemed so loud because of how quiet it was in the chapel.

My dad directed the family out the same doors to the limousine that would take them to the cemetery.

I've been to the cemetery tons of times with my parents, but I've never been to an actual burial. Dad always goes with the family, and sometimes Nate joins him, but my job is to stay behind and tidy up after the service.

Once the family had left, I opened the rear chapel doors. I stood there respectfully while the mourners filed out into the lobby.

Some lingered in the chapel, sitting with their heads together, speaking quietly. Not everyone would go to the cemetery. Some people probably had to go back to work or wherever.

"How are you doing, Evie?" my mom asked as she came up and gave me a side hug.

I looked up at her. "Okay, I guess. That was really sad." She nodded. "It was."

"The Katzmans sound like really nice people."

"They do. I wish I could have met them." She squeezed my shoulders. "I was thinking we could go to the service tonight at the shiva house and pay our respects. How would you feel about that?"

After a Jewish funeral, the grieving family sets up daily receptions and prayer services at someone's home for the whole week after the funeral. That gives everyone a chance to come and pay their respects. They often bring or order in meals so the family doesn't have to worry about cooking. There are prayer services every night too. I'd never been invited to go before now. It felt like a big deal, maybe part of my junior funeral director training.

"Okay," I said, nervous and a little excited. It meant a lot that my parents were starting to treat me like a grown-up.

"I bet Oren would be glad to see you," Mom said, giving me another squeeze. "Oh, by the way, Mr. Silver said that Oren will definitely be going to Beit Sefer in the fall—eighth grade."

Which meant he'd definitely be in my class. Beit Sefer has just one class per grade.

"Oh," I said with a shrug. "Okay."

Mom looked at me and was about to say something more, but some ladies in the lobby were waving to get her attention.

I guessed it was a good thing about Oren going to my school. Not that I was looking to make friends with him or anything. I was never doing that again. But even though I didn't think he liked me very much, at least he hadn't called me any names or told me I smelled like death.

So that was an improvement.

Eight

A couple of weeks after the funeral, I was at the dining-room table, surrounded by my craft supplies as usual. I was getting nothing done though. My meadow picture remained unfinished. I was completely uninspired. I'd spent hours and hours on it already, so why did I suddenly want to crumple it up and toss it in the trash?

Ever since I'd given Oren that special pack of tissues and he'd blown me off, quilling felt pointless. I had gone to the shiva house the night of the funeral, but he hadn't even come out of his room. Mom had reminded me that he was having a rough week and that he just needed time. Of course he was. I knew that. The worst week imaginable.

But I wanted to *do* something! I wanted to help him and make everything better for him.

How did my parents handle these feelings of helplessness?

I didn't even want to look at my project anymore. But

if I threw it out, my parents would find out and want to know why. Instead I packed everything into my big plastic bin. I'd figure out a way to get rid of it later. I was about to take it up to my room when my dad came in.

"What's up, Evie?"

I shrugged. "Nothing much."

"Well, in that case, I have some errands to run. Care to join me?"

"What kind of errands?" I asked suspiciously. The last time I had gone to "run errands" with him, I'd gotten stuck at the car license-renewal place with him for what felt like eternity.

"To the garden store and the cemetery to drop off some paperwork."

I scrunched up my face. I mean, I like my dad and all, but neither of those things sounded fun.

He raised an eyebrow and added, "Oh, and a quick stop at The Big Scoop. Would that help persuade you?"

Ice cream? Why yes, that certainly did help. But I had to be sure. "No car-license place?"

"Nope," he said. "Not this time."

I was still pretending to make up my mind when he took the bin from my hands and placed it on the table. Then he put an arm around my shoulders and turned me toward the front door. "Come on. I'm restless, and I feel like ice cream. It's been slow next door—a good thing, of course—but I've caught up on my paperwork, the roast is in the oven, and I don't have much to do."

Neither did I, since we hadn't had a funeral since the one for Oren's parents. When there are no funerals, there's not much to do over there, so I have to do extra chores around the house to earn my wage.

It is sort of weird that while we don't *want* people to die, when no one does we have no work to do. But I guess that's the life of a funeral director—you never know when you'll be busy. You have to be ready at any time. Sometimes Mom and Dad get calls in the middle of the night and have to get out of bed, put on their suits and go to work.

"All right," I said. I didn't really feel like going to the garden center or the cemetery, but ice cream makes everything better.

Our first stop was the cemetery. As we pulled into the lot, the car's tires crunched over the gravel. Dad parked in front of the groundskeepers' little house.

I used to think it was weird that Sarah and Richard— a really nice older couple—live in a cemetery, but when I asked Sarah about it once, she grinned and said she didn't mind because at least the neighbors are quiet.

It's a good thing they're there to keep watch over things. Not to warn us of zombies or ghosts, but to be there in case of *real* problems. Recently some jerks vandalized another Jewish cemetery in the next town, where there aren't people keeping watch. The vandals knocked over gravestones and even spray-painted some hateful symbols too. It was on the news, and made me sad and angry. Mom and Dad were really upset about it too. Sarah and Richard arranged for extra security lights and cameras to be installed, just in case.

"I'll just be a minute," Dad said as he grabbed the car-door handle. "You can wait here, 'kay? If you come in, Sarah will start talking, and we'll never get the ice cream."

I would have gone with him to say hi, but he'd made a good point. Sarah likes to talk even more than I do.

"Okay," I said, "just leave me the keys so I can listen to the radio.

Dad turned the key so that the radio and air-conditioning stayed on. Then he got out and walked up to the house.

I saw Sarah answer the door and gesture Dad inside. A song I liked came on the radio, so I turned it up and sang along.

The next song wasn't as cool, so I turned the radio down and looked around. What was taking Dad so long?

I scanned the sea of headstones, relieved that none had been knocked over and there were no signs of vandalism. But then something caught my eye.

Squinting, I quickly realized that the something was Oren. His right arm was still in a sling. He was wearing beige cargo shorts and a black Batman T-shirt. He was standing in front of two graves without stone markers.

Even from a distance, I could tell by the way his shoulders were slumped and his body was shaking that he was crying.

I'd thought about him a lot since the funeral, wondering how he was doing. My parents had visited the shiva house a few times after that first time I'd gone, but they hadn't seen him either. Shiva was officially over now, but even though the official week of mourning was done, nothing about Oren's life would go back to normal. It never would.

I got out of the car, and started toward him. It was a while before he noticed me and looked up. His red, teary eyes widened in surprise. I suddenly worried he was going to run away.

"Hi," I said with a little wave, thankful that he didn't look like he was about to bolt. "I...uh, I'm not following you or anything. I'm just here with my dad. He's having a meeting." I pointed my thumb over my shoulder at the little house.

Oren didn't respond or even nod. Instead he looked back down at the ground. Was he praying for me to go away?

I stared down too, focusing on the strips of new green sod that the groundskeepers had laid over the new graves. Even though they were covered up, I knew Oren's parents were underneath the grass. Obviously, Oren did too.

"Is your uncle here?" I asked, looking around but not seeing anyone.

Eyes still trained on the ground, Oren shook his head.

I wanted to hug him, but figured he'd probably hate that. So I stepped forward and offered him the packet of tissues I had in my pocket. I held my breath as I waited for his reaction. He looked at my hand for a second before he nodded and took them from me.

"Are you okay?" I asked.

He stared up at me like he couldn't believe what I'd just asked.

I replayed it in my mind.

OMG, Evie! Why would you ask that? He's at a cemetery looking at his parents' graves. Of course, he's not okay! He might never be okay!

"I mean…" I had to fight tears, wishing I had a time machine for my mouth. Why did I always say the exact wrong thing? "Shoot. I mean…um…do you like ice cream?"

He looked shocked.

"Ice cream," I repeated and took a deep breath to stop the tears. "Do you like it?"

He didn't answer right away. I noticed that his face looked a lot better than when I'd first met him. The bruises under his eyes were almost gone. Now they were sort of a pale yellowish green. And the cut down his right cheek looked a lot less…Frankensteiny. Not that I was going to tell him that. But I was glad he was healing. His arm in the cast looked the same, but I hoped it was getting better inside too.

Finally he nodded. It would have been so awesome to hear him actually say "yes," but at least he was communicating.

I looked over my shoulder just in time to see Dad coming out of the house. "My dad and I are going for ice cream, and I'm sure he wouldn't mind at all if you came with us."

Oren glanced over toward the house and then at me. He shrugged and nodded.

Yes! "Awesome," I said. "Come on!"

He glanced back at the graves.

"I mean, if you're done here," I added, trying to sound more serious again, like I did when I was at the funeral home.

He started walking with me toward the car, so I guessed that was his answer.

"Hey, Dad," I said as we approached. "Is it okay if Oren comes with us for ice cream?"

Dad smiled at me and then at Oren. "Of course. Oren, do you need to call your uncle to let him know where you are?"

Oren nodded and pulled out his cell phone.

Whoa! Was he going to call his uncle and actually talk to him?

He started texting.

Oh. I guess not.

As I waited for him to finish his text, I opened the car door so he could climb in.

Oren slid the phone back into his pocket, looked up and froze. His eyes became as big as saucers, and he swallowed hard.

"Hey, you know what?" said Dad quickly. "We can walk to the ice cream place. It's not far."

Why would we walk? It was so hot out. Oh! I suddenly remembered what had happened to Oren's parents. Maybe he was scared of cars now. I guess I couldn't blame him. He probably just needed some reassurance.

"My dad's a really good driver," I said. "He's very cautious and follows all the rules and speed limits. You'll be very safe, I promise."

"Evie," Dad said, putting his hand on my shoulder. "That's enough."

I frowned up at him. "But you told me we should always face our fears. Like when I fell off my bike, you said that I needed to get back on right away or I'd always be scared." I shrugged. "Now I ride all the time."

"Evie," Dad said sternly. "This is different."

I didn't think so. I mean, okay, yeah, having your parents die and breaking your arm and having two black eyes was worse than skinning your knees and cutting your chin. But it wasn't *really* different. Just a whole lot worse.

I had opened my mouth to say so when Oren suddenly rushed past me and hopped into the car.

"Are you sure, Oren?" Dad asked. "You don't have to— we can walk."

Oren shook his head and gave us what he probably thought was a smile. It looked more like a terrified grimace, but at least he was trying.

"All right," my dad said. "If you're sure."

I was about to remind Oren to buckle up, but he was already on it, pulling the strap across his chest and clicking it into place. I was closing the door and was about to get in the front beside Dad but instead decided to sit in the back beside Oren. Just in case he got scared and wanted to hold my hand.

He didn't.

Nine

We had planned to go to the garden center next, but once we were in the car, Dad said that errand could wait for another day.

When we got to The Big Scoop we could see it was busy. Dad dropped us off at the door so he could go park the car.

"See?" I said as Oren and I went inside to stand in line. "My dad's a very good driver."

He didn't say anything.

I was sure he would finally have to talk to the teenager behind the counter though. How else would she know what his order was? I was really looking forward to hearing his voice.

When it was our turn, Oren stood in front of the ice cream case and pointed at the mint–chocolate chip. He then held up his left hand with one finger raised.

"One scoop?" the server asked.

Oren nodded.

"On a cone?"

Another nod.

Would he ever talk again? I snuck a glance at him as he watched her lean into the freezer case and scoop his ice cream. It hadn't been that long since the accident, but he seemed okay. It wasn't like he was lying in bed, sobbing and devastated. Although... I *had* just found him crying at the cemetery, so he wasn't 100 percent okay. Still, right now he seemed almost normal—other than the not-talking thing.

"When did your uncle go back to work?" I asked him.

He tore his eyes away from the ice cream case to look at me. He frowned. I figured it wasn't very nice of me to try to make him talk.

I thought about how hard it must be for him being in a strange place where he didn't know anyone. His entire life had changed, in every single way.

"So you're by yourself all day?" I couldn't help myself.

"Here you go," the server said, reaching over the counter to hand Oren his cone. "One scoop of mint–chocolate chip."

Oren nodded at her in thanks. The server smiled back and then asked me what I wanted. I ordered a scoop of Cookie Dough—my favorite—on a cone. I turned back toward Oren. "So what are you going to do for the rest of the summer?"

Without looking at me, he shrugged and started licking his ice cream.

I was getting frustrated with the shrugs and the nods. I was about to say that maybe he could actually *tell* me about his plans for the summer when Dad came in.

"Hey, kids," he said. Just seeing him made me back off. I knew he wouldn't approve of my nagging. I even answered him in my head. *Yes, yes, I know, Oren has been through so much and I need to be patient. But being patient is hard and takes forever!*

"One scoop Cookie Dough," the server said as she handed me my cone. She turned to my dad. "What can I get you, sir?"

He ordered a banana split. "Don't tell your mother," Dad said to us, winking. "Besides, bananas make it health food, right?"

Such a dad joke. The server didn't laugh, but I did see the hint of a smile on Oren's face—the first one I'd ever seen.

Maybe *I* could get him to laugh. Everyone likes jokes. Sam and I had shared the same dorky sense of humor and had always told each other jokes. Sometimes we'd laughed so hard that tears came out of our eyes and our stomachs hurt. I didn't think I could make Oren laugh *that* hard, but still.

Oren's phone binged in his pocket.

He placed the cone awkwardly into his injured right hand and tugged his phone out of his shorts with his left. He fumbled with it a little, and I was worried he was going to drop it. I was about to offer to help or be ready to catch it when his shoulders slumped as he looked at the screen.

"What's wrong?" I asked, a bit scared. What more could happen to this kid?

He turned the phone toward me so I could read the screen.

Must work late. Sorry! Can u make sandwich for yrself?

Obviously it was from his uncle, and it meant Oren would be alone for dinner.

"Come to our place," I blurted out.

Oren just stared at me.

"For dinner," I said. "I mean, if you want to."

He looked over my shoulder toward my dad, who was still waiting for his banana split. "I'm sure it's okay," I said. "We have people over for dinner all the time." Which wasn't exactly true, but still, I knew my parents would be fine with it.

"And don't worry. I'm not, like, trying to force you to be my friend or anything," I explained. "It's just so you're not alone."

When he frowned at me, I added, "I don't have any friends. And that's just the way I like it."

Oren kept frowning, but I wasn't about to start telling him about Sam. Definitely not here anyway. Plus, I barely knew him.

Finally he took a long breath and nodded. He started to tap out a response to his uncle. It was pretty awkward to watch.

"Why don't you finish your ice cream first?" I said, pointing at the dribble of minty green ice cream running down his cast. "People might start to think you have some kind of gross infection." I made a face and pretended to gag.

Oren giggled. He actually *giggled*!

See? I was right. Ice cream really does make everything better.

Ten

Dad was cool with Oren coming for dinner, like I knew he would be. Once we finished our ice cream, he drove us home. As we were getting out of the car, I noticed Oren looking across the parking lot at the funeral home. His jaw clenched.

Sometimes I forget that when other people come into Walman Memorial Chapel, they aren't thinking about keeping the fridge filled with water, vacuuming the carpets or making sure the bathrooms are clean. They definitely aren't thinking about who dusts the caskets and the pews in the chapel. They probably don't even think about how those things *need* dusting.

When most people go there, it's because they have lost someone close to them.

Obviously that's what Oren was thinking about now.

"Come on inside," I said quickly, pointing in the opposite direction, toward my house. "We can watch TV until dinner or something."

He followed me to our side door. There were two sets of steps on the landing, one that went up to the kitchen and another that led down to the rec room. Dad had gone up, but once we were inside, I kicked off my shoes and led Oren to the basement.

I could hear Mom and Dad above us, getting started on dinner.

"Do you like corned beef?" I asked Oren as we sat on the couch.

He shrugged.

Great. *More* shrugging.

"Does that mean yes or no?"

Another shrug. It was getting really annoying.

"Have you ever had it before?"

He shook his head.

"Oh," I said. "Well, Dad has been brining the brisket for a week. And I can smell it cooking, so I know that's what we're having for dinner tonight. You'll probably like it. It's Dad's specialty. It's really delicious. So is the cabbage he makes to go with it. But there will be potatoes and carrots too, if you don't like cabbage. Not everyone loves cabbage. My brother, Nate won't touch it. But he'll eat twice his share of potatoes. The carrots are my favorite."

I reached for the remote and turned on the TV, happy that a fun talk show was just starting. My cat came thumping down the stairs. He sauntered into the room, his white tail aimed at the ceiling, and stopped abruptly when he noticed it wasn't just me on the couch. He is mostly white with a few markings, including a black mustache on his face that makes him look very fancy. He is quite a distinguished cat, as a matter of fact, other than when he licks his butt. Obviously.

Oren looked from the cat to me.

"That's François," I said.

Oren raised his eyebrows. I guess it *is* a funny name for a cat.

"Actually, his *real* name is Frank—Nate named him when I was too little to have a say. But look at his mustache. Don't you think a cat with a mustache should have a fancier name than plain old *Frank*?"

Oren stared at me for a second and nodded.

I guess that settled it for François. He jumped up onto the couch and settled right in Oren's lap.

"He likes you," I said. "And that's saying something, because he doesn't like almost *anybody*."

I saw a bit of that smile I'd seen in the ice cream shop.

"Do you have any pets?" I asked, even though I was pretty sure I knew the answer.

Oren shook his head. I was about to remove François, who isn't just distinguished-looking but also quite pushy sometimes. But Oren lifted his good hand and tentatively started petting the cat. Which, of course, had been the cat's plan all along.

After a while Dad called us up for dinner. This was a good thing, because I'd completely run out of things to say to Oren.

I know, that's hard to believe. I *never* run out of things to say.

But Oren and I had been sitting there without talking for so long that he'd even fallen asleep at one point. Which was a relief, because if he was sleeping, I didn't have to keep thinking of things to say to keep the conversation going. All by myself.

Anyway, when Dad hollered with our five-minute dinner warning, I led Oren to the bathroom so we could wash our hands. I caught myself telling him all about the different fragrances of soaps we have in the house (unscented for Mom and Dad's bathroom, lavender for the guest one and the one I share with Nate, and lemon curd in the kitchen).

Seriously, that's what our conversation had come down to. Soap smells.

Once we were done, I led him to the kitchen. The table was already set with an extra place. We were just about to sit down when the doorbell rang.

Mom glanced at Dad. "Expecting someone?" she asked. He shook his head. We get a lot of funeral-related phone calls during dinner, but never someone at the door.

"I'll see who it is," said Mom as she pushed back her chair.

A minute later she returned with Oren's uncle. "Natan," she said to my brother, "can you set another place? Oren's uncle will be joining us."

"Hi, Mr. Silver," I said with a wave.

"Hi, Evelyn," he said. "Good to see you. You can call me Jared though."

I smiled back at him. "And you can call me Evie. I hope you're hungry!" I glanced over at Oren. He seemed happy to see his uncle, but unsure at the same time. It occurred to me that he maybe didn't know his uncle very well. And now he was stuck with him as his sort-of dad.

It must be so weird for him. Jared seemed nice, but still.

Jared tugged at the striped tie around his neck. "It's very kind of you to invite me to dinner. I don't want to be any trouble though." He was wearing a suit, but not a dark funeral-type one. I wondered if he worked in an office. Or a bank. "I didn't have to work as late as I thought I'd have to. I figured you'd be done eating by now, to be honest. I didn't show up early just to wangle a meal out of you."

Dad laughed. "Wangle or no, it's no trouble at all. We were just about to start."

"And there's plenty. Ben always cooks for an army." Mom laughed as she put her hand on Jared's arm. "Truly, we're happy to have you."

While my brother set an extra place, I went into the dining room and grabbed another chair. I wedged it between Nate's spot and Mom's. Then I tucked a napkin under his fork. Leave it to my brother to forget the napkin.

"Thank you," Jared said as he dropped into the chair. He smiled at my brother. "You're a gamer?"

Nate frowned and then looked down at his shirt, which had some sort of nerd video-game logo on it. "Oh," he said, laughing. "Yeah. Do you play?"

Jared nodded. "I have been known to. I was thinking of taking Oren to the new VR place by the mall. Have you been?"

That was Nate's favorite place on the planet. His eyes lit up. "Oh, yeah! It's really cool. You'll love it!"

I glanced at Oren. He looked...not so excited. His uncle must have noticed, because his smile disappeared. He swallowed hard and then pasted a smile back on his face, though it didn't seam as real as the one from a moment before. "Anyway. Whatever we're having smells amazing. I thought dinner tonight was going to be a bowl of cereal."

Mom grinned. "That's all Ben. His famous corned beef and cabbage."

Dad smiled and passed around a basket of sliced challah before he led us in singing the hamotzi. I wondered if Oren's family had normally done the blessing over the bread before meals. Jared seemed to know the words. Oren, of course, said nothing.

Mom and Dad talked more than usual during the meal, mostly about our upcoming camping trip. I suspected they were trying to keep the conversation light. Oren and Jared gobbled up the second helpings Mom dished onto their plates.

Oren seemed interested in the talk about the trip. More than he had been about the idea of going VR gaming.

"Do you like camping?" I asked him.

His eyes went wide, and all of a sudden he seemed panicked. I didn't know what that was about, but I decided not to press him. I'd give him the space he needed. At least, I would try.

"I don't think Oren's ever been camping," Jared said with a smile. "Have you?"

Oren shook his head and looked down at his plate. Something was going on, but whatever it was, Jared didn't seem to be in on it. Trying to stick with my new vow, I didn't push.

Instead I told them about Danielle and how she and her family were traveling around in their big RV. I even described the inside of the RV so they could picture the bunks and the kitchen and everything. I would have told them all about the bathroom too, but Mom said that was enough and that they got the idea.

At the end of the meal, Jared pushed his chair back from the table and patted his full belly. "That was exceptional," he said. "Honestly, the best comfort food I've had in a very long time."

Oren nodded, which made me happy.

"Thank you so much," Jared continued. "Both for

looking after Oren this afternoon and for this." He waved down at his empty plate. "I…it's been a bit of a challenge now that shiva's over and I'm back at work and…" He darted a glance at Oren and sighed. "I've been on my own for a long time, and I'm not much of a cook. Having this—a normal meal with a family—means more than you know. To *both* of us, I think."

I looked over at Oren, but he'd dropped his head, and all I could see was his hair falling forward over his eyes. He'd done a good job of cleaning his plate, but maybe the reminder that he'd never have a family dinner with *his* family ever again had just hit him.

"Evie," Mom said. "Why don't you take Oren upstairs to see your paper project?"

WHAT? No!

After his reaction to my craft project, the last thing I wanted to do was show Oren my quilling stuff.

I was about to protest, but Mom glared at me. "Evie, please," she said. "Give us a minute. We'll call you when it's time for dessert." Her voice made it clear—it was time for grown-up talk. I was about to ask if she was going to kick Nate out too, but he muttered something about his favorite game and then disappeared.

I swallowed a sigh and pushed back from the table. "Come on, Oren."

Without a word—obviously—he slid off his chair and followed me. But instead of going upstairs to my room, I led him back down to the basement.

I flicked through the channels until I landed on an old repeat of *Jeopardy*, one of my favorite shows. Dad and I sometimes watch together and compete to see who knows more stuff (it is almost always him, but I am getting better). Oren's eyes seemed to light up, and he nodded when I asked if he liked it too.

What a relief that I wouldn't have to struggle to find more things to talk about.

Just as the show was ending, Dad called us upstairs for dessert.

"Lemon meringue," I told Oren as we started up the stairs.

We were almost at the top when my brother pushed past us. "Later," he said as he hurried out the door.

I looked at Oren and rolled my eyes. "He's probably gone to Nerdvana—it's a local comic-book store where he hangs out with his friends." I looked at Oren's Batman shirt. "Maybe we can go there sometime."

Oren nodded, looking like it was actually something he'd want to do.

Maybe comics were more his thing than VR gaming. I tucked that away for later.

The pie was already on the table, with one piece missing. Nate must have inhaled his before he ran out.

Mom was dishing the rest out onto plates. "Do you want some, Oren?" she asked.

He nodded.

I looked at him as he sat there, politely draping his napkin in his lap and waiting for everyone to get their pie before he even picked up his fork. His parents must have taught him his really nice table manners. That thought made me sad.

"So we've been chatting," Dad said, interrupting my thoughts. "And we came up with an idea that we're hoping you kids will be on board with."

I looked from Dad to Mom to Jared and then back to Dad. "What kind of idea?"

Dad smiled. "We were thinking that with Oren's... situation, and his being new to town and his uncle's busy work schedule, perhaps Oren could spend his weekdays here."

"What do you mean *here*?" I asked.

"He could walk here, or I would drop him off before I went to work, and he would spend the day with you," Jared said. "You could show him around town, and he could even help you out with your chores and things. If you're both okay with it, it would really help me out."

Mom nodded. "It would give you two the chance to get to know each other better before Oren starts at your school in the fall. What do you think?"

At first my heart did a little happy flip at the idea. To have someone my age to talk to during the days. But then I thought about spending all day, *every* day, with a boy who never speaks. Yes, my mom would say I can talk enough for two people, but that doesn't mean it's fun. I want to talk *with* someone, not *at* them.

Today had been a peek into what the rest of my summer would look like. Of course, I still wanted to be respectful and give Oren time until he was ready to talk, but what if that was never? I looked at my mom. She tilted her head at me and frowned. Clearly she was expecting me to jump at the idea. Then I remembered that my plan was to never have a friend ever again anyway. So what did I care if Oren never talked?

I glanced at Oren. He nodded, which was surprising. I had figured he'd come with me that afternoon because of the ice cream. Or because he had nowhere else to go. He didn't want to be my *friend*, did he? I sure hoped not. Even so, I couldn't be mean to him—he'd just lost his parents, had gotten really hurt and had no one. Of course I would be nice to him.

"Fine." I turned toward Jared. "We're both okay with it."

I just hoped Oren didn't think it meant we were going to be friends.

Because we weren't.

Eleven

The second my eyes blinked open, I remembered. Today was the first day that Oren would be coming over.

We'd have the whole day together until his uncle picked him up after work.

Dad had promised to take us to a movie in the afternoon, which would be fun. Also, a movie meant a couple of hours where I didn't have to figure out what to talk about.

I glanced at the clock on my nightstand. 7:19. Still lots of time to have breakfast, take a shower and get dressed before he arrived.

I threw off the covers just in time to hear the phone ring. Not my cell phone, but the house phone.

Someone had died. Because the only people who ever call that early are people who need my parents to help them with a funeral.

I slid my feet into my slippers and opened my bedroom door, listening. I couldn't hear any voices, so I shuffled into the bathroom that I share with my brother. He's a late sleeper—especially in the summer, when he stays up playing video games after everyone else goes to bed—so, unlike during the school year, I almost never have to wait for the bathroom in the morning. Some days I don't even see him until dinner.

Once I was finished in the bathroom, I went downstairs just as Mom was ending the call. She was still in her fuzzy slippers and penguin pajamas, but I could tell she was already in funeral-planning mode.

"Who died?" I asked as I tugged the fridge door open.

Mom sighed. "An older lady who lived at a long-term care home. You wouldn't know her."

I took out the carton of orange juice and put it on the counter before grabbing a glass. "How old was she?" I always hope for a really high number.

"Ninety-four," Mom said. She came over and gave me a side hug and a kiss on the top of my head. "She lived a good, long life. Had a big family with lots of kids, grandkids and great-grandkids."

"When's the funeral?" I asked.

"I'm not sure yet," she said as she glanced up toward the ceiling. "Your dad's in the shower right now, but he and Syd will have to go to the care home to pick her up. I'll be meeting with the family later this morning, and the tahara will probably be tonight." She paused. "Oh, darn it. That means I'm going to have miss book club again. Oh well. I hadn't finished the book anyway. Let Nate know when he wakes up that we'll need him to update the website as soon as we have details."

"I will," I said. "I guess this means Dad won't be taking Oren and me to the movie later?"

"Probably not, Evie," she said. "I'm sorry. We all have to make sacrifices sometimes."

"It's okay." I was disappointed, but it wasn't like my parents bailed on stuff for no reason. It was part of the job. If I was going to be a funeral director, I had to get used to that. "We'll figure out something else to do."

She was quiet as I poured my juice. Too quiet.

Once my glass was full, I looked up at her. "What?"

"Just—"

I finished her sentence for her. "Don't talk his ear off. I know, Mom."

"It's not that," she said. "Well, that's part of it. But just remember, it's only been a short time since the funeral. Don't expect too much from him, okay?"

I snorted. "If you mean don't expect *him* to talk *my* ear off, I won't."

"What I mean," she said, her voice a little stern, "is don't expect him to be eager to play or do everything *you* want to do. Take it easy on him."

The movie would have been perfect, but...

"Or...you could...hmm." She looked up at the ceiling again. "Why don't you see if he wants to try paper quilling? Or you could get out Nate's easel and paints. Doing something like that might make him feel better.

A lot of therapists use art to help grieving kids express themselves and sort through all the difficult feelings."

I knew that already. But even if it was a good idea, there was still a big problem.

"Mom, his right arm is in a cast, and he could barely eat with his left hand last night. He won't be able to paint." *And he probably thinks quilling is ridiculous.*

"Oh," she said, cringing. "You're right. I forgot about that. Well, whatever you do, just maybe let him decide. It's possible he'll just want to watch TV and chill out all day. That's all right too."

"Okay," I said, returning the juice to the fridge.

"Just..." she said and then stopped.

Now what?

"You know...sometimes you can get...persistent."

"I get it, Mom," I said, trying not to get mad. "I'm chatty *and* bossy!"

"Knowing is half the battle," my brother said as he shuffled into the kitchen.

"Shut up," I said, putting my hands on my hips. "Jerk."

"Okay, you two," Mom scolded. "I haven't even finished my coffee." She reached for her mug. "What are you even doing up, Nate?"

My brother pushed his fingers through his messy bed-head hair. "Dad's taking me golfing this morning," he said.

"Oh, I'm sorry, honey." Mom shook her head. "We just got a call."

Nate knew what that meant. Without another word, he turned around and started back toward his bedroom.

"We'll need you to update the website later," Mom called after him.

He grunted in response. Mom shook her head.

"Are all teenagers like zombies?" I asked. "Am I going to turn into one too?"

Mom laughed. "Let's hope not."

I made myself some peanut butter toast, got dressed and then found a spot in the living room to watch for Oren to arrive.

Mom and Dad were still upstairs getting ready, so when he came walking down the street, I jumped up and opened the door so he didn't have to knock or ring the doorbell.

He was wearing a green T-shirt with some sort of superhero emblem on it.

"Hi!" I said.

He gave me a wave and a tiny smile. I stood back and gestured for him to come inside, closing the door as he kicked off his sneakers.

"We can't go to a movie today, unfortunately," I said. "So we'll have to figure out something else to do instead. Mom said I should let you decide."

He stared at me for a long moment and then shrugged.

It is going to be a loooong day.

"TV?" I suggested.

That got me another shrug but also a nod, so I led him toward the stairs.

Just then Dad came around the corner in his suit. "Good morning, Evie," he said and then noticed we had company. "Oh hey, Oren. Great to see you. Sorry about the movie—we'll have to go some other day. But luckily you've got the whole summer ahead of you."

Oren nodded.

"Okay, Evie, I'm heading next door to get the..." He glanced at Oren and then back at me. "To pick up Syd and...Ecto."

It was nice of him to work around the word *hearse* so Oren wouldn't get upset. He didn't seem to notice.

"Okay," I said. "Bye, Dad. Come on, Oren."

Once we got to the basement, we sat down on the couch. I grabbed the remote. "It's a weekday, so mostly talk shows right now. Unless there's something you want to watch. We could try to find a movie on Netflix."

Oren shrugged.

I sighed.

And then I remembered what my mom had said. "Sorry," I muttered. "It's just...it would be a lot easier if you could tell me what you want."

He nodded. For a second I thought he was finally going to speak.

Instead he pulled out his phone and held it up before he started tapping away at it.

"You know, it would be a lot easier if you would just talk," I said.

He stopped typing and looked up, narrowing his eyes as he shook his head slowly.

Okay, message received.

"Sorry," I said again.

He held the phone up to me.

Lets go outside.

I jumped off the couch. "Okay. Like...gardening? Or a walk or something?"

gardening sounds fun

I didn't agree. In fact, I hated gardening and grumbled every time Mom asked me to pull weeds out of our flower beds. Why had I even mentioned it? *Think before you speak, Evie!*

But then I got an idea. "How do you feel about weeding?" I asked. Maybe this could work out after all. He could do something he liked, and I wouldn't have to do as much of something I *didn't* like.

He shrugged.

"Okay, cool," I said. "Come on, we'll need to put on sunscreen first so we don't burn. Last year I got burned so bad, I got blisters."

He nodded.

Then, as he stood up, I noticed his cast. His very white cast that was sure to get dirty in the garden if we didn't do something about it.

I pointed at it. "I guess we'll need to figure that out too."

Twelve

Mom came into the kitchen as we were putting sunscreen on our faces. She had traded out her pajamas for a navy-blue skirt and jacket over a pink blouse, with a pretty blue-and-burgundy scarf tied at her throat. She looked ready to meet with a family. Someday I'd dress up when *I* met with families, so I always paid attention to how she put herself together.

"You look really nice, Mom," I said.

That made her smile. "Thanks, Evie. What are you kids up to?"

"We're going outside to do some gardening."

Mom's eyebrows went up, and she looked at Oren. "You up for this?"

He nodded, even as I said, "Uh, Mom, it was *his* idea! It sure wasn't mine. You know how I feel about gardening."

Mom laughed. "Good point. Those beds out front could use weeding. But don't you get that cast dirty," she warned Oren.

"He won't," I assured her.

"I'm heading next door," she said. "I'll be back for lunch by one."

"I'll make lunch," I offered. Because fixing lunch was way better than gardening.

She smiled and poured herself another cup of coffee. On her way out with the mug in her hand, she gave me a kiss on the cheek. "Have a good morning, you two. Try not to track too much dirt back inside."

"We won't," I assured her.

Once we were done with the sunscreen, I offered to wrap Oren's arm so it would stay clean and dry. Thanks to Nate's busted leg the previous summer, I knew a trick for keeping a cast from getting dirty.

I went to the kitchen junk drawer and got out a plastic shopping bag and a roll of duct tape to seal it up. As I returned to him with my supplies, I noticed he didn't have any markings on his cast yet. My brother's had been filled with doodles and signatures from his friends. By the time he got it taken off, there wasn't a square inch that didn't have scribbles or pictures drawn on it.

Of course, Oren's situation was a lot different. Also, I got the feeling he hadn't been back "home" since the accident. All his friends were still in his old town. Did that mean none had come to visit him?

Maybe he hadn't just lost his parents, but all his friends too. Or maybe, like me, Oren didn't have any friends to begin with. Not to say I have *never* had any friends. But since the thing with Sam, and with all the jerks at school, I'm better off without any now.

I told Oren all about Nate's soccer accident and how after a kick he'd come down wrong and snapped the bones in his lower leg.

Oren cringed, especially when I told him how they said a bone had even poked out of his skin. For some reason, it's one of Nate's favorite stories to tell. How gross it must have been to see his own bone sticking out like that. I'm glad I didn't see it, because I would have puked for sure.

When I was done with Oren's arm, we grabbed a ball cap for him and Mom's big floppy gardening hat for me from the coat closet and headed outside into the sunshine.

I took him around to the front flower beds, and we got to work. Well, *he* got to work. I went to the shed to get the rake and the shovel thing that I use to dig up weeds. When I returned, he already had a pile of yanked-out weeds beside him.

"Oh, I'd better get the wheelbarrow," I said and returned to the shed. I had to move the hose and the bag of mulch to get to the wheelbarrow. Then I noticed a giant bag of fertilizer. I took some time to read all the information on the label, even though it wasn't very interesting.

By the time I got back to Oren, his pile had become a mountain.

"Wow," I said. "You're doing great! Even with just one good hand!" He gave me a shrug. I gathered up all the weeds and put them in the wheelbarrow.

I figured I couldn't let him do it all on his own and was about to kneel down beside him to help (really, I was!) when he wiped off his forehead with his plastic-covered arm.

"Thirsty?"

He nodded.

"I'll be right back," I said.

Instead of getting us plain water, I took the time to mix up some lemonade, getting the sugar just right, and poured it into two big glasses with lots of ice. Nate came into the kitchen then, so I made him a glass too.

I followed him back to his room to remind him that he needed to update the website.

"Mom hasn't sent me the details yet," he said as he sat at his computer desk and pulled up the funeral home website. "But I guess I can start a post. Do you know anything about the person who died?"

"No." I shrugged. "Just that she was ninety-four."

I stood there for a while, leaning against the door frame. Nate swiveled his chair and looked at me. "Shouldn't you be outside with your friend?"

"He's not my friend." I pointed toward the window and made a face. "But he's happy out there weeding."

Nate snorted. He knows how much I hate weeding. He probably hates it just as much. "You shouldn't make him do all your work, you know, whether he's your friend or not."

"He likes it!" I protested. "It was his idea!" Well, sort of.

"How's he doing, anyway?" my brother asked as he took a sip of his lemonade.

"Better. But still…" I shrugged.

Nate nodded. "So brutal for him. It's nice that you're hanging out with him," he said, adding, "even though you're making him do your chores."

"Not all of them!"

He turned back to his computer and pulled up the funeral notices, scrolling through them until he found the one for Oren's parents. He read it and shook his head. "That really sucks."

"I know."

Nate swiveled back toward me. "You should go out there."

I glanced out the window. Oren was kneeling and hunched over, tugging at a big dandelion. He didn't look unhappy. "In a minute."

Nate finished his lemonade, got up and came toward the door, handing me his glass. "I'm going to grab a shower. By the time I get out, you'd better be back out there."

"Okay, *Dad*," I said, rolling my eyes.

After Nate left, I dropped into his chair and read Oren's parents' funeral announcement. I'd seen it before, but now that I was getting to know Oren, it was more meaningful. They weren't just his parents—they were real people. They'd had jobs and loved to travel. They'd been his family and now they were gone.

SORRY FOR YOUR LOSS

Not wanting to get all emotional, I went back to the list of old notices—people I didn't know at all. They were arranged by last name, and some were really old—Dad never deleted them in case family members wanted to look up the records later.

I read a few, losing track of time. Some were notices of funerals I'd attended in the last year. But most were old records. One in particular, from several years ago, was *very* interesting. I tucked the information away in my brain for later.

"EVIE!" Nate barked when he came into his room, wrapped in a towel, his hair wet and messy from the shower.

"I'm going!" I jumped up and ran out of his room. Stopping in the kitchen, I added some fresh ice to the two glasses of lemonade and took them outside.

By this time the wheelbarrow was full, and Oren had moved around to the side of the house where Mom's herb garden was. Good, because that needed weeding too.

He wasn't working though. He was sitting on the grass, staring at the funeral home. There wasn't much to look at—Mom was inside, probably meeting with the family or getting ready to. And Dad had left with Syd in the hearse and would probably be a while. I hoped so—I didn't really want Oren to have to see Dad and Syd bringing a body into the funeral home. They were always wrapped up in sheets or a special plastic bag, and Dad and Syd were always very respectful, but even if you were used to it, like I was, it could be weird to see, knowing what was in there. For someone not used to it, it would probably be pretty scary.

I sat down next to Oren and handed him one of the glasses "Here you go. I hope you like lemonade."

He nodded and took the glass, the ice cubes clattering as he took a sip.

"Are you okay?" I asked softly. "I mean, I understand if it's weird being here after..." I waved toward the funeral home.

He shrugged and looked down at his glass.

What did that shrug even mean? I was getting to know him but not well enough that I could interpret all his different shrugs.

Finding a flat spot on the ground, I put my glass down before I pulled my phone out of my pocket and opened up a note.

Can you please tell me if your okay?

I turned the screen toward him so he could read my message.

He took a long drink of his lemonade and put his glass down before he took the phone from me and frowned at it. Then he typed something and aimed it back so I could read his message.

You mean you're

It took me a second to figure out what he meant. I looked up at him. "Are you seriously correcting my grammar right now?"

He shrugged again, but his lips were twitching—he was trying hard not to grin.

I rolled my eyes and shoved my phone toward him. "Here," I said. "Give me your number."

He entered it in, and a second later I heard his phone bing. He handed mine back to me and then pulled his out of the big side pocket of his shorts. A second later my phone binged too.

Now you have my humber.

I laughed and typed back, **I think you mean NUMBER.**

He smiled over at me for a half a second and then returned to tapping a message. **I do feel weird about being here. But want to know.**

I looked up at him. "Want to know what?"

He waved toward the building.

What happens in there. He took a deep breath. **Like, to my parents.**

I read his message over and over, trying to figure out exactly what he meant.

Finally I said, "You mean you want to know what my parents do with people who have…like…people who have died?"

He nodded.

"Not like…" I took a breath. A long, deep breath. "You don't want to see a dead person, do you?"

He took a deep breath too. Then he nodded again.

My stomach jumped at that. "I don't know, Oren. I mean, they don't even let me see everything. *I've* never even seen…"

He frowned and went back to typing.

When he finished, he looked up at me, tears welling up in his eyes.

My parents died. I deserve to know.

Oh. After a minute I said, "Does this have to do with why you won't talk?"

He shook his head.

"If I take you over there and show you stuff, will you talk?"

Another head shake.

"Will you at least tell me *why* you won't talk?"

That got me head shake number three. So much for that idea.

Please, Evie?

It was the first time he'd used my name. Even though it was in a text message, for some reason it made it impossible for me to tell him no. Maybe he needed to see what went on behind the scenes to begin dealing with his grief.

"All right," I said. "I'll take you in there and show you everything I can. Even...yeah. Okay. If you are sure you really want to."

He nodded.

"We'll have to do it when my parents aren't around," I said, knowing that my parents would absolutely 100 percent *not* be okay with it. Even if it was my mission to help Oren this way, they wouldn't get it. Or why it was so important to me to give him what he needed to help him heal.

I looked over at him. Something was different. He looked...relieved.

Which told me he was nowhere near as freaked out as I was. To distract myself, I started yanking weeds out of the herb garden, but a second later my phone binged.

Why don't you want any friends?

I looked at him. Was he asking because he wanted to be my friend?

A tiny part of me wanted to tell him about Sam. But most of me chickened out. I shook my head and returned to the giant dandelion in front of me. "It's complicated," was all I could bring myself to say.

Thirteen

Once we finished weeding the herb garden, we went inside to make lunch. I was going to make tuna sandwiches, but when I grabbed the loaf of bread and asked Oren if that sounded good to him, he made a face and shook his head.

"Do you hate tuna?"

He shook his head.

"You hate tuna *sandwiches*?"

He made another face that included a stuck-out tongue.

"Oh really," I said, hands on my hips. "You think you can do better?"

He nodded. Emphatically.

My eyebrows went up. "You some sort of gourmet chef or something?"

He shrugged and pulled out his phone.

Not a pro, but I like to cook.

"Fine then, Guy Fieri," I said, sweeping my arm around the kitchen. "Have at it."

He actually smiled at that. *Challenge accepted!*

I have to admit I was impressed. Not just impressed, but *really* impressed. Because even one-handed, Oren had taken the cans of tuna I'd opened and turned them into a fancy dish of stuffed red and orange peppers. He'd even sprinkled cheese on top and added a garnish of dill and parsley from Mom's herb garden before I put them in the oven.

I'd helped him with a few things, but he did most of it. While we waited for the cheese to melt, I kept thinking about how he wanted to go next door and see everything.

Everything.

I hadn't even seen everything. Obviously, I would have to someday if I was going to be a funeral director. But that was years away.

I wasn't sure Oren was ready to see it all. He probably didn't even realize what he was asking me to show him.

Once you see things, you can't *unsee* them. Ever. Maybe instead of showing Oren a dead person, I could teach him everything I know about funerals and what happens to people when they die. I know tons about all that stuff.

Then Oren wouldn't have to get all freaked out about what he could never unsee. I wanted to help him, not make things worse. I had a feeling that being a good funeral director sometimes meant protecting people from what they didn't realize would hurt them.

I snuck a look at him as he checked on the peppers. I remembered that his uncle had said Oren had been having nightmares. I wondered if he still was. I didn't want to be responsible for making him have more.

Maybe he did have a right to know what had happened to his parents at the funeral home. But I could *tell* him all that. I could even show him *almost* everything. Like the caskets and even the special room where the bodies are prepared.

Of course, I'd only show him that stuff when there *wasn't* a dead person in there.

The peppers were done, the table was set, and I was mixing up more lemonade when Mom and Dad came in from next door. Mom looked at the platter of stuffed peppers in the center of the table and then at me.

"Not me," I said, pointing at Oren. "*I* was going to make plain old sandwiches."

"*You* did this?" she asked Oren. "It looks amazing!"

"You never told us you were a chef," Dad added playfully.

Oren shrugged and smiled.

"He used to do a lot of cooking," I said. "At home with his family."

There was a sudden silence in the room. One glance at Oren told me I'd screwed up again. I didn't even know if what I'd said was true—I'd just assumed he had and wanted to be included in the conversation. *Ugh, Evie!*

Mom cleared her throat. "Well, this looks great. Thank you, Oren." Then she got a weird look on her face. "Do you mind...I mean...would it be okay if..."

"Diana," Dad said.

She huffed at him and looked back at Oren. "Would it...could I...would it be okay if I gave you a hug?"

Oren took a deep breath and then nodded. He looked...not quite scared and not exactly weirded out either. But sort of like he wanted the hug but wasn't sure if he should.

Mom stepped toward him slowly. Like she was hugging a porcupine, she gently put her arms around him. Then, without warning, Oren launched himself against her. He hugged her so hard that she grunted in surprise.

"Oh, honey," Mom said, her voice cracking as she pulled him in tight. Really tight.

That's when Oren began to cry. Like, *really* cry, until I could hear him wailing. I thought I'd have been happy to hear a sound from him, but not like this. It was probably the worst sound I'd ever heard.

Tears sprung to my own eyes. Oren was clinging to my mom like he was never going to let her go.

"Evie," Dad said softly, putting his hand on my shoulder. "C'mon, let's give them a minute."

We left the kitchen and went into the dining room. Then Dad said, "Why don't you run upstairs and tell your brother to wash up for lunch. And you can tell him

I have the details of the funeral for him to put up on the website."

"When is it?" I asked.

"Tomorrow," he said. "Her family is in town, so they can do it before Shabbat."

"Right," I said. You can't have funerals on the Shabbat, which started Friday at sundown.

Dad gave me a nudge toward the stairs. "Go on. Get your brother. I'll make sure Oren's okay."

I glanced toward the kitchen. I heard more sobbing. Poor guy, I thought. It made me absolutely, 100 percent sure that Oren definitely wasn't ready to see *everything* that went on next door.

Which, to be honest, was a relief.

Fourteen

The next day was the funeral for the ninety-four-year-old lady from the care home. Her name was Mrs. Rubin and, according to her obituary, she was the loving wife of Herbert, mother of four, grandmother to seven and great-grandmother to three. She loved to knit and play mahjongg and was a longtime volunteer for Meals on Wheels. She seemed like a nice lady, and I felt a bit sad that I never got to meet her.

At dinner the night before, Dad had told us this funeral would be a large one with lots of mourners, but that the family had decided they wanted it to be graveside only. The whole service would be at the cemetery. Mrs. Rubin's family didn't want a big, somber event inside a building on what was looking to be a beautiful summer day. Mrs. Rubin's daughter had said her mom would have liked that—to have everyone gather in the sunshine to say their final farewells.

Having her funeral at the cemetery meant there wouldn't be a service in the funeral home at all, so

I wouldn't have to be there. In other words, I had the day off. It also meant that by the time Oren arrived at my place, my dad would already be next door, getting everything ready for the funeral, including putting Mrs. Rubin's casket into the hearse so he and Syd could drive it over to the graveyard.

I was just finishing my orange juice when there was a knock at the door. I looked up at the clock—it was nearly nine already. A glance through the peephole told me what I already knew. It was Oren at the door. He was carrying something in his hands, covered with tinfoil.

I opened the door and waved at Jared as he pulled out of the driveway.

"Hi! Good morning, Oren," I said.

As usual, he nodded.

"What's this?" I asked, pointing at what he was carrying. I stepped back so he could come inside.

He kicked off his shoes, and as he went past me, I could smell what he was holding. And it smelled like heaven. If heaven were made of cheese.

I led him to the kitchen, where he put the glass dish gently onto the counter. He struggled a little with his cast as he put his arm back into the sling.

Once he had done that, he took out his phone and began tapping at the screen. A second later mine binged.

It's to thank your family. For everything.

"That's really nice of you," I said, meaning it. "Thank you so much."

Mourning families who were sitting shiva often got dinners cooked for them by friends and extended family. Sometimes Dad even made up meals to take to a family that didn't have a lot of visitors. But it wasn't very often that *we* got something. Especially something that smelled so delicious. Oren and his uncle must have gotten a lot of meals if they had something left over even after shiva had ended.

Oren shrugged and tapped out another message.

You've all been really nice. So I wanted to make something for you. It's mac and cheese.

Wait. *He'd* made this dish? I shouldn't have been surprised after he'd whipped up those tuna-stuffed peppers. But I was still impressed.

"Mac and cheese is my absolute favorite," I said. His big smile made me suspect it was his too.

Even though I'd just finished breakfast, my mouth was watering already. I wanted to grab a fork and dig in. But he'd said it was for my family. Mom would not be happy if she opened this up later and saw half of it missing.

"Let's put it in the fridge," I said as I yanked open the refrigerator door. "I'll just make room."

Right then Mom appeared in the kitchen doorway. She was dressed in her funeral suit. "Hi, kids."

"Mom," I said. "Look! Oren made us an entire tray of mac and cheese as a thank-you."

Mom's eyes went wide as she looked from me to Oren to the dish. "You did? As a thank-you for what?"

"Because we've been nice and for the funeral and everything," I said for him.

He nodded.

"You didn't have to do that," Mom said.

I could see her waterworks were going to start up again. Time to do something before it got weird.

"But it's a really big tray, so maybe we should invite Oren and his uncle for Shabbat dinner tonight to help us eat it." Even though I sort of wanted to eat the whole thing on my own. Right now.

"Oh," Mom said, reaching for the coffee pot. "That's a good idea. Oren?"

He held up his phone.

"He'll text his uncle," I said.

He nodded again. I was really getting to know him and what he wanted to say.

"Great," Mom said as she finished filling her mug. "I need to go now so your dad and I can head to the cem—service," she said. "What are you kids up to today?"

Well, I was planning to take Oren next door to look at *some* stuff—the more boring things probably, but I couldn't tell Mom that. "Not much," I said with a shrug. "Maybe some more gardening or something."

"Speaking of gardening," Mom said. "Since we don't need you next door, can you go down to the garden store? Mr. Lansky has a box there for us."

"Are you sure? I mean..." I darted my eyes toward Oren, who had no idea why it might be awkward for us to go.

Thankfully, Mom seemed to clue in. She bit her lip. "Oh. Right…uh…good point. But it's just clay pots."

My phone binged. A text from Oren.

Let's go!

"All right then." I shrugged. "I guess we're going to the garden store."

"Good." Mom opened up her wallet and took out a twenty-dollar bill. "Here you go. Get some ice cream on the way home. Your dad and I won't be home for lunch, but I'm sure you two won't starve."

Her right eyebrow went up. "Should I bother telling you to fix yourselves something *other* than ice cream?"

"Probably not," I said. "Anyway, bananas make it health food, right?"

Mom rolled her eyes and laughed. "You are so your father's daughter," she said as she went out the door.

Fifteen

As soon as Mom was gone, I grabbed a couple of shopping bags and the hats we'd worn the day before. I handed Oren his and put the other one on my head. I was strapping on my sandals to walk to the garden store when my phone sounded. I pulled it out and read the text. It was from Oren, even though he was standing right behind me.

Will you show me?

I didn't pretend not to know what he was talking about. I turned and looked at him. "You sure you still want to go next door to see…stuff?"

He nodded. But he looked scared at the same time.

"You're absolutely sure you want to see *everything*?"

He took a long breath and nodded again.

"Fine," I said. "But we have to go to the garden center first. If I don't get the pots, my mom will be mad. And don't forget ice cream." It was never too early for ice cream.

He nodded again and then we were on our way. It was already hot out, and I was glad we'd put on hats before we left.

I was going to tell Oren the reason for the clay pots on the way to the store. But the more I thought about it, the more I didn't want to. Not just because what my parents used them for was weird, but mostly because if he asked me the reason, I wouldn't be able to answer. The truth was, I didn't really know why. It was a tradition or a law or something.

But yeah, also kinda weird.

So instead I filled the time talking about random stuff.

After a while I got sick of listening to myself.

Not that Oren seemed to mind.

We were barely a step inside the garden center when we were hit by the air-conditioning. I lifted my face up to get the full effect of the cool air coming at me.

The walk home would be even hotter. Ice cream was a for-sure, but maybe we could run through the sprinkler in the backyard later. We'd have to be careful with his cast, but I would just wrap and tape it up again like I had before. I was a pro at that.

I was just about to make the suggestion when I heard my name.

I turned away from the blast of the air-conditioning to see Rabbi Alisha, my favorite teacher, smiling at me. She was wearing cute capri pants and a pink shirt with sunflowers on it. I liked her outfit, but I was used to seeing her looking a lot fancier. It felt weird to see her dressed so casually, like it did the time I saw my fourth-grade teacher in yoga pants, shopping at the grocery store. She was like a whole different person!

"Hi, Rabbi Alisha!" I said, giving her a big smile. "I love your outfit! What are you doing here?"

"Thanks." She smiled back at me. "I'm getting a few more tomato plants for my vegetable garden. How about you?"

"We're here to pick up some clay pots." I glanced over at Oren. "This is Oren, by the way. He—" I stopped, not sure how to introduce him. I didn't want to mention his parents, and I couldn't exactly call him my friend. "He's...this is Oren." When I darted a glance at him, he was watching me with a tiny smile on the right side of his mouth, like he thought it was funny I was struggling.

I huffed at him a little but turned back to the rabbi. The way she smiled at him, with her tilted head and scrunched-up eyebrows, told me she knew he'd lost his parents. "Nice to meet you, Oren," was all she said.

He nodded back at her.

If it seemed weird to her that he didn't speak, she didn't let on.

As I was thinking this, Oren tapped my shoulder. I looked at him. "Yeah?"

He pointed to the back of the store where the pots were.

"Okay, sure," I said. "I'll be there in a sec." I watched him walk away and then turned back toward the rabbi.

"How's he doing?" she asked quietly.

For a second I wondered if I should tell her that he wanted me to show him things at the funeral home. I sort of wanted to because she'd probably have some good advice. So I almost blurted it out. But then it occurred to me that she might tell my parents. They would *not* be happy.

"He's okay." I shrugged. "I guess. I mean, he's still not talking, so…"

Rabbi Alisha tilted her head. "Give him time. It hasn't been very long."

I sighed. "That's what everyone says. I mean, I get that he's sad, but other than the no-talking thing, he seems fine."

"What people show us on the outside may not be a very good indicator of what's going on inside," she said and then gave me a sudden side hug. "Be patient with him, Evie."

I sighed.

Rabbi Alisha laughed, like she could read my mind. "But you're doing a good thing, being a friend to him."

But I *wasn't* being a friend to him. Yeah, I was hanging out with him and teaching him things and letting him help with my chores, but we definitely weren't friends. I felt like I should be doing *more* to help him. Like, if I was doing a better job, he'd be speaking by now. But if I said that to Rabbi Alisha, she'd only remind me about patience. Again.

"Just be there for him. I'm sure he'll come around, but you can't rush grief. It has its own schedule for everyone."

"I know," I sighed.

"Anyway," she said. "I have some old prayer books I need to bring over for burial, but I'll talk to your parents tomorrow to arrange a time."

When I stared at her, trying to figure out what she'd just said, she laughed and explained. "Old, worn-out siddurs can't be thrown away because they have God's name in them. They need to be buried in the cemetery out of respect. There's a special spot for books and other holy objects. We haven't done it in a while, but I'm running out of space keeping them at my office."

"Oh, that makes sense," I said, even though I had never heard of burying books at a graveyard. "Do you have to put them in a casket?"

She shook her head. "No. Just an old sheet or pillowcase is fine. Anyway, maybe I'll bring them over this weekend. I'd love to see some of your quilling projects."

I almost groaned, wishing I'd never told her about my artwork. I'd been excited to tell her all about it when it was going so well. Now? Not so much. Ever since Oren's terrible reaction to the gift I'd made, I had hardly any interest in quilling.

"Great," I said. "But I'd better get back to Oren."

She smiled at me and wished me Shabbat shalom.

When I found Oren, he was carrying a wire basket in his good hand. "Hi," I said and craned my neck to peek inside the basket. There were four shiny, painted clay pots—blue, pink, yellow and green. The green one had a yellow sunflower on it.

"Are you planning to make a windowsill garden?" I asked. "Plant some herbs for your cooking?"

He looked down at the pots and then back up at me, frowning. Then he held the basket toward me.

"Oh," I said as I realized he'd picked out the pots for me. "No, I mean, thanks. No offense, and those are nice and all. But I need plain pots without any paint or anything on them. Just the regular old orange clay ones."

His frown got even…frownier.

There was no getting around it now. "I'll explain in a minute. But here." I took the basket from him and returned the pots to the shelf before I put the basket down. "Come with me." I led him toward the store's office in the back of the building. The door was open, and Mr. Lansky—the store's owner—was sitting at his desk, looking at his computer.

"Hi, Mr. Lansky," I said to get his attention.

He lifted his head and smiled at me. "Why, hello! How are you doing, Evelyn?"

"Good, thanks. This is Oren. We're here to pick up the pots," I told him. "Mom said you had some for me?"

He grabbed a box on the corner of his desk. "Yes. Right here."

I stepped into the office and held open my shopping bag with both hands, so he could place the box directly in it.

"Awesome, thanks!"

Mr. Lansky laughed as he made an embarrassed face. "I dropped a box of brand-new pots when I was stocking the shelves last week. At least they're useful for something."

I noticed Oren looking from Mr. Lansky to me. He was very confused.

He waved me off when I pulled out the money Mom had given me. "I can't sell broken pots, especially to your parents. No charge."

Now Oren looked *really* confused. I realized he probably thought we had come to buy regular pots. Like, unbroken pots for planting stuff in. But nope. The box Mr. Lansky had given me was full of broken pieces of pottery.

There were so many pieces, in fact, that I wouldn't have to buy any whole pots just to break up. Which meant Oren and I could *both* get banana splits if we wanted.

I'd have to explain it all to Oren later.

"Thank you," I said to Mr. Lansky. "We'd better go."

"Nice to see you, Evelyn. Say hi to your parents. Nice to meet you, Oren," he said before he turned back to his computer.

"Come on," I said to Oren, who was still looking very confused. "I'll tell you on the way."

But as we walked out of the store, I wasn't sure how to explain. Maybe I shouldn't have promised to show him things at the funeral home. If I didn't know how to tell him about the pots, how was I ever going to show him the other stuff? The really serious stuff? The *scary* stuff?

I knew we were supposed to face our fears, but this felt different.

We'd gotten about twenty steps from the store when Oren poked my arm and pointed at the shopping bag. "Oh, you want to carry it?" I asked.

His left eyebrow went up like he was saying, *Nice try!*

"Fine," I sighed and then blurted, "They're for the funeral home."

Now *both* eyebrows went up.

"You sure you want to hear about it?"

He inhaled and nodded.

"You won't be able to unknow it if I tell you," I warned. "And it's kind of creepy."

He blinked twice and nodded again.

"Last chance," I said.

He exhaled loudly in frustration. Okay, so he was *really* sure.

"All right." I swallowed and began. "After they put the...person...into the coffin, they put pieces of clay onto their face. One piece over each eye and one on the mouth, three pieces."

His eyes went really wide and his mouth formed an O. Then he reached into his pocket for his phone.

"Before you ask," I said, "I'm not totally sure why. Something symbolic. But I do know it has to be plain clay—pieces from the painted ones aren't right." I quickly added, "Even though the ones you picked out were really nice."

He tapped at his phone and then turned it toward me.

Have you seen how they do it?

"No," I said, shaking my head. "I've never done a tahara—that's the name for the special ceremony they do to get the person ready for the funeral. They have to say a bunch of prayers and do everything in a very specific way and order."

He nodded and then looked down at his phone for a long moment. I wondered if he was glad he hadn't seen his parents in their coffins. Or maybe he wished he had. Dad says everyone is different—some people want to see, others don't. I wasn't sure yet which side I was on.

I was afraid to ask Oren though.

Suddenly he started typing again.

So do you think that's where "potty mouth" comes from?

I giggled and then covered it up with a cough. I didn't mean to laugh—we were talking about serious stuff! But I'd been surprised—that was *not at all* what I'd expected him to ask.

"I don't know," I said. "Probably not." When I looked up at him, he was smiling. "Oh, I get it," I said, rolling my eyes. "That was a joke."

His grin got wider.

This was what I'd meant when I told the rabbi Oren seemed fine. But he still wasn't talking. It was so weird.

"Funny," I said. "Anyway, now you know."

Thank you.

"You're welcome."

His smile disappeared.

But I want to know more.

I sighed. "You're sure? The clay pots are nothing. It gets weirder. Scary even."

You promised.

"I know," I said. "But I want to make sure."

I'm sure. I want to see it all.

Did he though?

Did *I*?

Sixteen

I didn't speak for nearly ten minutes. After I'd promised again that I would take Oren to the funeral home to show him around, I didn't know what to say. Finally, though, as we got closer to the ice cream place, the silence became unbearable.

"So how do you like living with your uncle?" Not my best, but it wasn't like *he* was coming up with sparkling conversation.

He shrugged.

"He seems pretty nice," I said.

He nodded.

"Were you close before the...um...before?" I asked, even though I knew they hadn't been.

This time he shook his head.

"You knew him though, right?" I asked. "He wasn't a *total* stranger, was he?"

Another head shake. Then he sighed.

"You're going to like our school," I said, quickly

changing the subject. "We don't just do regular school stuff but also archery and even Israeli folk dancing in gym. It's really fun."

He gave me a weird look. Maybe he didn't like folk dancing.

Or maybe he was worried he wouldn't make any friends. *I* still didn't want any, but I supposed it would be okay to have him in my class.

"I'll make sure you don't end up sitting anywhere near Miri or Sasha."

His eyebrow went up.

"Remember I told about the jerks at school who call me names? Miri and Sasha are the worst of them. Truly horrible human beings."

He tilted his head. I was getting so good at reading him. That was his "Oh really?" look.

"Totally. The worst."

I could tell Oren wanted me to elaborate. I fidgeted for a moment. "They're just so mean. They call me names like Corpse Girl and say I smell like death." I had to swallow because a big lump had formed in my throat.

His eyes widened as his mouth dropped open. He pulled out his phone, tapped hard at the screen and then turned it to show me.

SO MEAN!

"I know, right?" I cleared my throat and went on. "I mean, I take showers and baths *all the time*. And I've never been close enough to a...I mean...I don't think

I—" The tears came out of nowhere. I dropped my head and let them roll down my face.

Oren put his good hand on my arm. When I just kept on crying, he squeezed until I looked up at him. He shook his head really hard and then started typing again.

You don't smell like death! You smell like strawberries!

"Thank you." I sniffed.

Why are they so mean?

"I don't know. They're just..." I sighed again. "I don't know. I thought it was because they didn't understand what my parents do. But when my dad came for career day, that made it worse."

Jerks.

"I mean, it's not like I even want friends, but..." I trailed off.

Oren's raised eyebrows said *Why?*

Could I tell him about Sam? I'd never told *anyone* about what had happened. Not Mom or Dad or... anyone. I'd never even said his name out loud since last summer.

I thought about what I already knew about Oren and how brave he'd been after everything *he'd* been through. I exhaled. "I did have one friend back at summer camp. He was really good at origami. But he's...we're not friends anymore. After that..." I shrugged. I couldn't look at Oren, couldn't tell him the rest. How after everything that had happened, I never wanted to have another friend. Ever.

How come?

"Drama," I squeaked out.

Oren nodded knowingly.

Kids can be such jerks!

I took a deep breath. "Anyway, since then I've been sort of a loner." How could I explain that it just hurt too much to try to make friends? "Doesn't matter. The other kids probably think I talk too much anyway. Or maybe that I'm not nice. Who knows."

You are nice!

I gave him the best smile I could muster. "Thanks."

And I think you smell nice too.

I grinned at him. "I'm nice enough that I might even let you try my ice cream. Come on."

I had a banana split. Oren did taste it, but only the strawberry and chocolate parts because he doesn't like pineapple. He had a brownie thing with vanilla ice cream and peanuts on top. I got to try it—it was good—but my banana split was better.

It was also way too big. By the time I realized I wasn't going to be able to finish it, I felt pretty full and gross. I threw the rest of the melted mess in the trash.

I grabbed the bag of clay pieces, and we left the shop and headed home. When we turned the corner to my street, I saw the hearse right away. That meant Mom and Dad were back from the funeral.

"I guess we can't go over today," I said, trying not to sound too happy about it. "Want to run through the sprinkler? I can tape up your arm again like yesterday so it doesn't get wet."

He looked down at his outfit.

"You can borrow a pair of Nate's board shorts," I said.

When we got into the house, I told him to wait while I went upstairs to my brother's room.

Thankfully, Nate was out of bed and was either in the basement playing video games or had left to meet his friends to...I didn't know what. Probably to play video games. I tugged open his dresser drawers until I found one with his shorts and shoved my hand in toward the back. The first pair I pulled out had Minions on it. I didn't remember him ever wearing them, so I doubted he'd care if Oren borrowed them.

"These okay?" I asked when I got back down to the kitchen.

Oren was sitting at the table. He shrugged and reached for them.

"You can use the bathroom. I'll change in my room and meet you back down here. Then I'll tape you up."

After I changed into my suit, I grabbed two beach towels out of the hall closet and returned downstairs. I grabbed supplies for his arm from the junk drawer before heading toward the bathroom and knocking on the door.

"Ready?"

When he opened the door, I put the scissors and tape down on the counter beside his pile of clothes and then turned toward him. "Those fit pretty good," I said, nodding toward the shorts he was now wearing. I tried not to stare at the bruises on his torso. I didn't succeed. They were yellow and green and mostly faded, but they covered almost his entire chest. I didn't know why it had never occurred to me that he might have more injuries than the ones I'd already seen.

"Do those hurt?" I asked before I could stop myself.

He looked down at himself and shrugged.

"I hope they're getting better," I said, suddenly feeling awful for even bringing it up. Like he needed a reminder? And obviously they were getting better. "Have a seat," I said, pointing at the closed lid of the toilet.

He sat down and held his cast out toward me. I made sure there were no holes in the bag and slid it over his arm. As I turned to get the tape, I noticed something peeking out of the pocket of his cargo shorts folded up on the counter.

Oren saw me looking. He reached up with his good hand and pulled the thing out of the pocket.

It only took a moment for me to realize what it was. I was so shocked, I just stared at the two little flowers I'd made for him. They were crumpled and worn, but there was no mistaking them. They weren't attached to the packet of tissues anymore. Maybe he'd removed them when the tissues were used up.

I looked at him. "What is this?"

He did a double take, confused.

"No." I rolled my eyes. "Of course I know what they are, but I thought you threw them out."

He shook his head and gently wrapped his fingers around the flowers as he pressed them into his chest. Right over his heart.

"So…wait." Tears sprung to my eyes. It was clear what he was saying without words.

Still I had to ask. "You *like* them?"

He nodded. Then he grabbed his phone and typed out:

I'm sorry I never thanked you.

"It's okay."

I keep them with me all the time. Even under my pillow at night.

I nodded, not sure what to say to that. After having thought he hated them, I was overwhelmed that the little paper flowers meant so much to him. I guess when I couldn't be there, my flowers were. That felt good in a weird way.

They want me to go to therapy.

"Who? The flowers?"

He snorted.

No. Uncle. Grandparents. They want me to talk to someone.

How would that even work? Would he type out his feelings in emojis or something?

"You know…" I cleared my throat. "You can always talk to me if you want to. I…I mean, I'm not a therapist, but like I told you when we first met, I'm a good listener. I'm also pretty good at hugs and I can—urk!"

Suddenly I was getting hugged. Hard. Even though he could only use his one arm, Oren was clinging to me as tightly as he had to my mom.

I could tell he was crying, too, so I just kept on hugging, using both my arms until he took a deep breath and began to pull away.

When the hug was over, I reached for a tissue because I was crying now too. I pulled one out for him.

We stood there for a few minutes, sniffling and blotting our tears.

"You okay?" I asked finally.

Oren shrugged and tossed the tissue into the bin before he typed some more.

Would you show me how you made them?

"You mean the flowers? Like, you want me to show you how to do paper quilling?"

Yes. Maybe you can help me make something like the flowers but bigger. Something I can keep forever.

I remembered what my mom had said about therapists using art to help kids work through their grief.

"What are you thinking? Like, a whole picture?"

He nodded.

"Totally! I can for sure help you!" That it might actually help him made me want to do it even more. "I'm working on a picture right now. It's got a meadow and other flowers and stuff. I can show you that and how to curl and glue the paper and everything."

Can we run through the sprinkler first?

I wanted to get started right away but I needed to go at his pace. If he wanted to run through the sprinkler, we should run through the sprinkler.

"Of course," I said, showing how patient I could be. "We can quill later."

After I taped up Oren's cast and we put on sunscreen, we went outside and turned on the sprinkler. We played around, running through the water and blasting Nate's water cannons at each other. We had so much fun that we didn't even realize what time it was until Mom poked her head out the back door and told us to turn off the water before we flooded the neighborhood.

When I looked down, my feet were squishing in puddles in the grass. Whoops!

"Also, you need to come get ready for dinner," she said. "We need a salad to go with that amazing mac and cheese."

"Five minutes," I called out just as I was hit with a stream of water from behind. "Ugh! He got me again!"

Mom gave me a look, but then smiled at Oren. She was clearly happy that he was having a good time, which made two of us. Three if you counted him.

"Fine," Mom said, pretending to be exasperated. "I'll do up the salad, so you can make it ten."

We made it twenty, but no one complained.

We went inside and dried off. By the time I had changed into dry clothes, Oren's uncle had arrived and was sitting in the kitchen.

"Hi, Jared," I said. "How are you doing?"

"Hey, Evie. I'm good, thanks." He gave me a weak smile.

He looked kind of awful. Not much different than he had on the day I'd first met him at the funeral home. But with neater hair. I felt bad for him. I figured it must be tough to have to go on doing normal things when your world has been shattered. I wondered if *he* was seeing a therapist. Oren had lost his parents, but Jared had lost his sister and was suddenly responsible for a kid he barely knew.

Oren appeared in the doorway. He was back in his shorts and T-shirt, his sling in place. I thought I might have time to show him my quilling stuff, but Mom told us it was time to get ready for dinner. Together Oren and I set the table.

The mac and cheese was amazing. Even Nate said it was as good as he'd ever had, and I could tell he wasn't just saying that to be polite. Jared was impressed too, and he told Oren that if this was an indicator of his cooking skills, he was welcome to take over in the kitchen anytime.

Oren nodded eagerly, like it hadn't been a joke. And when Jared scooped out a third helping of the gooey and so delicious pasta, I realized it really hadn't been a joke.

I didn't get to show Oren my quilling stuff after dinner either. Nate had barely cleared the dessert dishes before Jared pushed back from the table and started saying his goodbyes. He needed to get Oren home, he said. I think he really needed to get *himself* home, but Oren didn't fuss. I said I'd show him my quilling another time.

I walked them to the door. "Have a great weekend," I said.

"Thanks, Evie," Jared said with a small smile. He really did look exhausted.

"I had a good day," I told Oren as he put on his shoes.

He only nodded back, but I could tell he meant he had a good day too.

Seventeen

Saturday was Shabbat—the weekly day of rest. Since funerals can't be held on the sabbath, every week Mom and Dad have from Friday night to Saturday night completely off. And they take that time off *very* seriously. We always do something together on Saturday afternoons, powering down our devices and doing things old-school: board games, flying Dad's fancy kites in the park, checking out a museum or going to the JCC pool. Or sometimes we walk through the botanical gardens. Even though I hate gardening, I don't mind going there because I don't have to weed *those* gardens and, more important, we almost always stop at the ice cream store on the way home.

On this Saturday, Nate wanted to go to the pool because that's where his friends were. But he was outvoted, so we headed out to the gardens. We strode along the paths and through the big bushes of roses that were in bloom. I loved how their sweet aroma wrapped right around me. It felt good to be out in nature, smelling the flowers, listening to the birds and just being with my family. Even though the more we walked, the more my feet started to hurt—my sneakers were getting pinchy.

I told Mom all my shoes were getting tight. She laughed and told me to stop growing so fast. She promised to take me to the mall for new shoes soon. Then she leaned in close and whispered, "Maybe we'll get pedicures too, huh? A girls' pamper day? What do you think?"

I smiled up at her. "That would be awesome! Thanks, Mom."

She grabbed my hand and squeezed it. I took in a few more deep, rose-scented breaths. After everything Oren had been through, I found myself appreciating my family more. I tried not to think about what it would be like to lose them, but with Oren around so much, it was hard not to.

We stopped at the The Big Scoop on the way home. It was super crowded, so we took a number. As we waited for our turn, I looked around at the people in the store.

Oh no! At the counter was a familiar face. Sasha. She was holding two ice cream cones and was very focused on licking one of them. I looked around but didn't spot Miri, thankfully. Then I noticed an old man standing at the cash register next to Sasha. Maybe her grandfather? He looked a little familiar.

He took one of the cones from Sasha and started toward the door.

I turned away, trying to be invisible. I heard a deep, gravelly voice behind me.

"Hello, Ben, Diana."

Of course the man was coming up to say hello to us. My parents knew everyone.

I had no choice but to turn around.

"Hi, Jerry," Dad said.

Mom smiled. "Good to see you, Jerry. You're looking well."

"You know Nate, of course," she said as my brother nodded at the man. Then Mom turned to me. "This is our youngest, Evelyn. Evie, this is Mr. Kepler."

"Nice to meet you," I said politely.

He took my hand in his big one but thankfully didn't crush it. He gave it a polite shake as he smiled at me. "Lovely to meet you."

He turned toward Sasha and put his hand on her shoulder, nudging her forward toward us, even as she kept eating her ice cream and didn't look at me. "This is my granddaughter, Sasha." He tilted his head at me. "You look about the same age. Maybe you girls know each other?"

I nodded. "Yes, we are in the same class." *Unfortunately.*

Sasha huffed. "Zaidy," she said. "Come on, Mom's waiting for us in the car, and my ice cream is melting."

Her grandfather chuckled and gave Mom and Dad a

knowing look. "The princess has spoken. Good seeing you all," he said and then smiled down at me. "Nice meeting you, Evelyn."

"You too, sir," I said, making a point of not looking at Sasha even though I could feel her glare on me.

And then they were gone.

"Are you two friends?" Mom asked.

"Not even a little," I said.

She looked surprised. "Jerry's such a nice man. He lost his wife many years ago."

"He's on the chevra kadisha," Dad said.

That was why he looked so familiar. I must have seen him coming or going from the funeral home. It wasn't a secret group, but Dad said they didn't talk very much about what they did. It was important to be respectful and modest about their duties.

Finally we got our order—a banana split for Dad and me, a strawberry cone for Mom and a butterscotch sundae (with extra nuts) for Nate. We went outside and sat down at a picnic table. Dad sat beside me so we could share easily. I dug into the pineapple side first.

That made me think of Oren and how he didn't like pineapple. I wondered what he was doing right now. Would his uncle take him out for a family day? Would they go somewhere for ice cream? I sighed and dug into the chocolate side, slicing and scooping up a piece of banana with my spoon.

"You okay, Evie?" Dad asked.

I looked up at him as I realized he was talking to me. "Huh? Yeah."

"Thinking about Oren?"

I nodded. "Just wondering how his weekend is going."

"It's going to be a long process for him, settling in," Mom said. "His entire life has changed. But at least he has you—I think you're really helping him."

"I *want* to help," I said. So much.

Dad put his hand on my arm and squeezed. "You are. His life is unimaginably hard right now, and the best thing you can do for him is be there for him. He doesn't even have siblings to turn to."

I looked at my brother. He was completely focused on getting the last of his sundae into his mouth. He must have felt me staring at him and glanced up. "What?"

Dad snorted. "Nothing."

"What are you talking about?" Nate asked, looking at each of us suspiciously.

"Not you," Mom said. "We were talking about Oren. How he doesn't even have siblings to help him through this."

Nate turned his eyes on me. "Aren't *you* his new sister? Or are you more like a *girlfriend*?"

"NO!" I yelled. My face got hot.

"Natan," Mom scolded. "Don't tease your sister."

My brother made a face at me. "But she makes it so easy!"

I was about to say Oren was lucky not to have siblings, but then I realized that even though Nate was a giant pain, I would *never* want anything bad to happen to him. I would be devastated if anything ever did.

On the way home, Mom was humming to herself as we walked. It struck me as kind of weird that someone who had to deal with dead people all the time could be so happy.

"Hey, Mom?" I said.

She stopped humming and looked at me. "Yeah, hon?"

"Did you always want to be a funeral director?"

She laughed. "Not at all. I went to college for social work. I always thought I'd be a therapist of some sort."

"Wow," I said. This was the first time I'd heard that.

She nodded, smiling. "It's true. I thought maybe I'd work in a hospital." She shrugged. "Or open a private practice."

She glanced at Dad, who was up ahead. "And then I met a friend of a friend who was in the funeral business."

"Dad?" I asked.

"The one and only. We were dating by the time I finished school, and I was looking for a job. Then your grandfather died suddenly, and your dad needed help." She shook her head. "I told him I'd help out with counseling the families until he hired someone else."

"He never hired someone else?"

"I'm still waiting," she said with a laugh. "After a few weeks I knew I wanted to work there full-time. I also knew I wanted to say yes when your father asked me to be in his life full-time too."

I blinked up at Mom as the meaning of her words sank in. "Wait," I said finally. "Please don't tell me that he proposed to you in the funeral home!"

"No, he did not!" She was smiling at Dad, even though he couldn't see her. "I'm not sure I would have said yes if he had. He proposed in a fancy restaurant on the anniversary of our first date. Very romantic and appropriate."

"Oh good," I said, relieved that Dad hadn't done anything creepy. "Are you ever mad that you didn't end up becoming a therapist like you'd planned?"

Mom shrugged. "There's a lot of overlap between what I do now and what I thought I'd do. I always wanted to help people through counseling. I actually love that part of the job—I find it's the most rewarding."

I looked sideways at her. "I hear a 'but' coming."

"You are a very intuitive girl," she said, giving me a boop on the nose. "Overall I'm very happy and fulfilled by what I do. But the truth is, I don't always love the hours. Being on call all the time has its challenges—making plans, *breaking* plans."

"Yeah, like going to the movies!"

"Yes, I do know how hard it is for you kids as well." She gave me a sad smile.

I thought about how much she and Dad did for the funeral home. And for us. It made me feel a little guilty for grumbling.

"Still thinking you want to be a funeral director?" Mom asked a few steps later.

"I think so," I said, nodding. "I know it's a really important job. I want to do something that helps people."

Mom put her arm around me and pulled me in close. "I know you do. And I already know you'll be great at it. I can tell by how much you're doing to help Oren."

She was right—I did want to help him. But what she didn't know was that my desire to learn all about the funeral business hadn't started because I wanted to help Oren.

It had started when I was trying to figure out a way to help *me*.

Eighteen

I woke up early on Monday morning without even setting an alarm. I hurried to shower and eat breakfast, and then I brought my giant case of quilling supplies down to the dining room.

Today I was going to teach Oren how to quill, which, hopefully, would also be art therapy. Maybe if it made him feel good enough, he'd start to talk again. Yes, I know I was supposed to give him time, but quilling is seriously so relaxing that I was sure it would work. I was excited for my own projects again too. I'd never really thought of my artwork as meaningful, but since Oren had told me he kept the little paper flowers I'd made with him all the time—even under his pillow when he slept—I felt inspired to make something that was not just pretty but also, maybe, important too.

I unfolded my plastic tablecloth and spread it over the dining room table. Quilling can be very messy, especially for beginners, and Mom would lose her mind if I got glue on her antique table again.

I began to lay out all my supplies—stencils, scissors, glue, quilling tools, shapers and, of course, paper. All kinds of paper. Plain paper in all the colors of the rainbow, textured, deckled edges, glittery, vellum. I even had some shiny origami squares that I'd gotten from Sam tucked away. I'd never used them in my art though.

When Oren arrived, I led him into the dining room and pointed at a chair. "I've got everything set up. You can sit there."

He pulled his phone from his pocket and put it on the table before dropping into the chair.

It was then that I realized we were going to have a problem. Oren's right hand was still in the cast. Quilling is a two-handed job.

"Um," I said, suddenly feeling awful for having forgotten about his injury. It hadn't occurred to me that he wouldn't be able to use his fingers enough for quilling, which can be really fiddly. "So for the first lesson, you have to watch me doing it."

He looked at me very seriously. He had no idea I was making it up as I went along.

I grabbed my work-in-progress. "This is what I've been working on. It's a meadow. I just need to add a sun up here and a couple more flowers and then it'll be done. What do you think?"

Oren tilted his head.

"What?"

He grabbed his phone.

It needs something.

"Yes. It needs a sun. Here." I poked my finger at the top corner. "Like I just said."

No. Something more.

For a guy who knew nothing about quilling, he had some nerve! "What do you mean?"

Oren's eyes darted around the picture and then he started typing on his phone again. **Needs something on the side. Too much stuff on the bottom. Maybe a tree?**

"What are you? Some sort of art genius?" I demanded.

He stared at me until I wanted to fidget. Instead I turned my head and looked at my picture. I held it away from me and then *really* looked at it—critically, like Dad had said to look at the paintings when we'd gone to the art gallery one Shabbat.

"Huh," I said after a long moment of studying my picture as a piece of art. "A tree *would* be good," I admitted. "Where would you put it?"

He showed me with his finger, tracing it down the left side of the picture. I tried to visualize a tree there, with lots of browns and greens to offset the light grasses and colorful flowers. I liked the idea.

"You're right, Oren," I said. "And I'm sorry I sort of yelled at you."

He shrugged and started tapping at his phone.

Make the tree. I'll watch & learn.

I put the picture down and got to work on creating the tree. Oren helped me pick out the different colors and handed them to me just as I needed them, shades of brown and even some black and deckled-edge beige. Most of the trunk was made of long strips arranged up and down, but I also coiled a few dark pieces into knots to make it look rough and natural. Once the trunk was done, I made branches. Then it was time for the leaves. Thankfully, I had lots of greens in different shades too. Oren watched as I used my special comb tool to make tons of coiled ovals that I pinched to have pointy ends like teardrops.

Before I knew it, the tree was finished. I held it up. It looked amazing. Oren was so right—the picture had definitely needed a tree.

"We make a good team," I said.

"Hey, kids," Dad said, wandering into the room. He was still in his fleece pajama pants and a T-shirt. "What are you up to?"

"I'm showing Oren my quilling," I said as I proudly pointed at my project. "He helped me put in the tree."

"Great job, you two," Dad said as he leaned over to look more closely. "That's really great. It almost looks like a tree of life."

"Huh," I said, tilting my head to really look at the tree. He was right. It did resemble the silver pendant Mom sometimes wore, which was a tree with a rounded canopy of individual leaves. It represented wisdom and the Torah, or something like that. I'd always thought it was pretty. Maybe I'd made my tree like her necklace without even realizing it.

Dad had opened his mouth to say something else when the phone rang. He and I both went still, looking at each other. Oren continued assembling a pile of paper strips.

Mom answered the phone in the kitchen. "Yes, Syd. Of course," she said in her serious voice. "I'll send Ben to... oh...where? Yes. We'll get her transferred into our care right away."

Someone had died.

Without another word, Dad left the room.

I glanced at Oren, but he was still sorting papers. If he knew what was happening, he didn't let on. A moment later he looked up at me. He pointed toward the tree and then at the green and brown papers in front of him.

"You think it needs more?" I asked. "*Another* tree?"

He shook his head and picked up his phone.

I want to make one for my parents. A memorial tree.

"Like a tree of life," I said.

My name means tree.

Whoa. "Really? That's cool."

Oren looked around the room. His eyes landed on the stack of old, worn-out prayer books piled on top of the hutch that held our good dishes. Rabbi Alisha had brought them over the day before for Dad to take to the cemetery and bury.

Oren got up out of his chair and went over to the books, opening one up. The cover was so worn out, it nearly came off. He flipped through the pages before he turned back toward me and pointed. I was pretty sure he was saying, "What's up with these?"

I explained how you can't just throw out books with God's name in them, that they were waiting to be buried.

He returned to the table and picked up his phone.

Can we use them? They'd look cool in a tree trunk.

Huh. I'd never thought of that. I looked over at the books. They were just going to the cemetery to get buried because they were too worn out to use, so why not?

But I wanted to be sure. "We'd better ask my parents first," I said.

"Ask your parents what?" Mom said as she came in.

I pointed at the pile of books. "Can we use one of those for quilling? Oren wants to make a tree as a memorial for his parents."

Mom's eyes softened as she looked at Oren. "That's such a wonderful thought," she said. "But unfortunately, no, you can't use the books, for the same reason we can't throw them out. They're sacred texts and can't be cut up. I'm sorry."

Oren's shoulders drooped.

"What if…" She chewed on her nail.

"Mom!" I said. "What if *what*?"

Her back straightened. "Right. Sorry." She turned to Oren. "How about I print out a couple of the programs from the funeral on some of Evie's nice paper? They'd have your parents' names on them but aren't sacred texts. You could use those, and it would make for a beautiful memorial, I think. Would that work for what you want to do?"

"Like I did with the flowers," I said.

Oren nodded. His eyes got all watery.

I loved the idea. I grabbed my folder of blank sheets. "Which ones do you like?" I fanned out the pages for him, and he pulled out three. One cream card stock, a handmade beige papyrus with a deckled edge, and a sheet of thin vellum—three of my favorites. He had good taste.

"Okay, I'll go print them now." Mom took the pages from him and then turned to me. "Your father and I have to go out of town on some business. You two will be okay here? Nate's going to update the site and then he'll be heading out for the day."

"Yes, we'll be fine." I pointed at all the art supplies on the table. "We have lots to keep us busy."

"We'll be home later this afternoon, so fix yourselves some lunch. Call if you need anything," she said before she left the room.

She was barely gone when Oren aimed the screen of his phone at me.

Let's go next door.

Nineteen

A few minutes later Mom returned with the printed pages. Oren and I made strips out of them while she and Dad got ready upstairs. Well, Oren pointed out the words he wanted and then *I* made strips using my paper cutter, because cutting straight and even strips is a two-handed job. He had tried, but the result was basically a disaster.

While I cut, I explained the different techniques of coiling paper using the twirly tool, the special stencils and the combs to make the cool shapes. He'd already seen me do a lot of them for the tree, but some of them were complicated and had taken me a long time and some YouTube tutorials to perfect. Some I *still* had to do over and over to get just right.

While I rambled on, I was also thinking about our secret mission as soon as my parents left. It made me nervous enough that my hands shook a little, and I messed up some of the shapes. Oren seemed not to notice though.

Less than a half an hour later, everyone—even Nate—was gone from the house and we were alone. I was still fiddling with and talking about paper, but I could feel Oren's eyes on me.

"I just wanted to give them time to get the hearse and leave," I explained. "I'm ready now." Sort of.

No getting out of it now. I'd already decided I wasn't going to show him *everything*, but I was still nervous.

We put on our shoes, went out the side door and walked across the parking lot to the funeral home's back entrance. I was about to press the code into the keypad, but I stopped and turned back to Oren.

"Last chance. It's okay if you've changed your mind."

He looked a little freaked out, but he shook his head and pointed at the keypad.

"Okay, okay." I entered the code, and when I heard the lock release, I pulled open the door. I held it for him to go through, knowing the light would come on automatically. "There isn't...I mean, there aren't any...*people* in here. But I can show you around and explain stuff."

Once we were both inside, I pulled the door closed behind us and turned the lock. I was about to start down the hall, but first I asked, "So are you freaked out?"

He bobbed his head yes.

"There aren't any ghosts," I said. "If that's what you're worried about. I'm in here all the time, and I know for sure that zombies and ghosts aren't a thing. Dad says people say that spirits sort of hang around between the time they die and when they get buried, and maybe that's true. But I don't think it's like what you see in movies."

For a second I worried that it smelled weird in there, but when I took a sniff, it smelled like it always did—a combination of the wood polish I use on the pews and the cleaner for the bathroom and floor. Clean and lemony—not a smell you would associate with dead people.

Oren looked around at the walls and then up at the ceiling, which was dotted with lights spaced at regular intervals. It was like he was looking for something. Or maybe he was surprised that it was different than he'd expected. But really it was just a regular building.

Following his gaze, I noticed a cobweb up in the corner. No ghosts though.

"So where should we start? Do you want to see the inside of a casket?"

His eyes went wide, and then he pulled out his phone and poked hard at it before turning it toward me.

CASKET?!?

I shrugged. "It's just a wooden box lined with fabric inside. It's not scary if there's no one in it."

He didn't look so sure.

"There's a whole showroom full of them," I said, pointing my chin toward the front of the building.

Can I do that some other time?

"Sure. Come on then," I said. "I'll show you the fridge."

He followed along as I led him to the door marked Private. It opened to a storage room that regular people never got to see. When people come to arrange a funeral for a loved one, they go into the office to do the paperwork and then they go into the showroom to pick out a casket. Then, on the day of the funeral, they use the quiet room before the funeral is held in the big chapel with all the pews. There's no reason for them to go into the room where the supplies to do the taharas are kept.

I led Oren inside. "It's just a regular storage room. No big deal."

He stopped just inside the door. He frowned at the washer and dryer. It seemed normal to me now, but I tried to see everything the way he would, like when I'd come in here for the first time and thought it was weird to have a washer and dryer in a funeral home.

I gave him the same answer Dad had given me: "The people doing taharas wear lab coats and use sheets and towels. Things that need washing."

Oren nodded and continued looking around. His eyes landed on the racks of supplies. I watched as he scanned up and down the shelves. There were boxes of kippahs, black ribbons for family members to tear and wear on their clothes, cases of tissue packets, bottled water, toilet paper and cleaning supplies. He seemed interested but also unimpressed. Maybe that was a good thing.

"You okay?" I asked.

He looked at me and nodded before he tapped at his phone.

Where's the fridge?

I went over to the big stainless-steel door and pulled the giant handle. I held my breath as it opened.

I hid my relief when I saw that it was empty. I mean, I knew it should be, but...

Oren squeaked.

I glanced at him. His eyes were huge. I looked back into the fridge, but no, it was for sure empty.

"What?" I mean, I could understand if we'd opened the door to find there was a person in there, but we hadn't. No big deal.

He was still staring inside, but there wasn't much to see. It was like a giant, deep cabinet with three shelves. Each one had a handle, so you could pull it out, but otherwise it was just a giant, cold steel box. But it was clear what it was made for.

"What's the matter?" I repeated.

Finally he tapped again on his phone.

You said fridge!

"It *is* a fridge. That's where the bodies go when they come here. Jewish people don't do embalming, so we have to put the bodies in a refrigerator."

Oren swallowed, his eyes still wide with alarm. I was confused. He had *asked* me to show it to him! Maybe he didn't understand the process.

"Do you know what embalming means?" I asked.

He started to nod and then abruptly stopped, frowned and shook his head.

"Do you want to?" I asked. I didn't know a lot about it, but probably more than most kids.

He sighed and nodded again.

"It means putting special chemicals inside the person's veins so they don't…" I wasn't sure how to say it. "So they… um…don't…so they don't change. Like a preservative, I guess, before the funeral. Sometimes people don't have their funerals right away or they put the people in the casket but want to keep the lid open during the service. The bodies have to be embalmed for that to happen."

"WHA?" came out of Oren's mouth as it fell open.

It was the closest he'd ever come to talking. He must have been *really* freaked out.

I nodded. "Jewish people aren't supposed to do those viewings, but my parents told me that it happens at other funeral homes. Some people like to see their loved ones one last time."

Oren made a face.

"Anyway," I said as I shut the fridge door, "every culture has its own way. Jewish people don't embalm or cremate their dead, but they try to bury them as soon as possible. So the fridge is pretty important. But it's just a fridge, you know?"

Oren showed me his phone.

I thought you meant a fridge for bottled water or where your parents keep their lunch!

"OH!" I couldn't help laughing. "No, I mean, there's the little one in the quiet room, but my parents just come home for lunch."

Oren's look was saying, "Sure, I get it *now*."

I looked around the room, but there wasn't much else to show him. "There's more to see out there." I waved toward the back of the building. "But that stuff can be more...intense."

I took his frown to mean, "Like what?"

"The room where they do the taharas. Where they prepare the body for the funeral."

He cringed.

"It's okay if you don't want to see it," I said, "but it's not as weird as you might expect."

He lifted an eyebrow.

"No, really," I assured him. "The room is sort of like a doctor's office. A big sink and a table. I've been in there. Just not during a tahara. But it's not really scary."

Oren inhaled a big breath, then stared at me for a long minute before he typed his next message.

Maybe tomorrow. OK?

"Sure," I said, flipping off the lights and leading him back toward the door. "You did really good though. Is this the kind of stuff you wanted to know about?"

He frowned but nodded.

More please.

Just what I was afraid of.

Twenty

After Oren had left for the day and we had eaten dinner, my parents and I returned next door to prepare for Mrs. Eisen's funeral. Mom would be doing the tahara with some other female volunteers, and Dad would be finishing up the paperwork and making sure everything was ready.

Since there was a funeral the next day, I had some things to do too. Nate had plans with his friends, so he'd asked me to refill the box of kippahs. I was going to remind him that funeral directors had to cancel their plans all the time. But he would have said he had no intention of being a funeral director. Anyway, he offered to give me three dollars for the two-second job, so I didn't mind.

I grabbed the nearly empty kippah box and went into the storage room to get more. I didn't think men who borrowed them meant to take them home after funerals, but it happened a lot. Dad was always ordering more to restock our supply.

When I came back out into the hallway, my eyes went to the closed doors of the preparation room. The ladies were in there, doing the tahara. Other than the sounds of squeaky shoes on the floor—like in the school gym during basketball—it was quiet. I wasn't surprised that I didn't hear voices—the rules say you can't chat or tell stories because it's disrespectful to the person who has died. Maybe because they can't join in your conversation. I'm not sure if that is the reason, but I do know you can only talk when you need to or to say the special prayers, including one where you ask forgiveness in case you disrespect the person by accident.

So while the silence feels a bit creepy, the process is really respectful. My mom and the other volunteers take their jobs very seriously. They follow all the rules no matter what. They never make fun of the dead or say anything bad.

It was too bad all the jerks at my school—like Miri and Sasha—didn't follow those rules. I shook my head to push them out of my mind. I had more important things to focus on. I was learning how to be a good funeral director by getting a better understanding of grief. I knew I was a good listener, so I would able to help the families, like my mom did. But would I be able to do the other stuff, the preparation of the bodies? Or would I be too scared? Too emotional? Maybe even too grossed out? I mean, I didn't even like getting a paper cut. How would I handle it if someone had died after a bad accident like Oren's parents had? What would that tahara be like? What if—

"What's wrong?" Dad asked from behind me. He startled me so badly that I squeaked and nearly dropped the basket of kippahs.

"Oh!" I said. "I was just zoned out, thinking."

"C'mon." He nodded to the front of the funeral home. I fell into step beside him. "Thinking about what?"

I sighed as we walked around the corner. "Taharas. Like, what happens if it's…you know, bad. Like if there's…like a car accident."

He didn't answer right away. "You mean, like with Oren's parents?"

I nodded. Even though I was nervous to hear about them, I still wanted details. Oren did too—he kept insisting he wanted to know what happened to them.

Before he said anything else, Dad led me to his office and pointed at the seat in front of his desk.

"What exactly do you want to know?" he asked once he had settled into his big leather chair.

I took a couple of breaths and looked down at my hands. "Is…is it…gross?"

He didn't say anything at first. I lifted my eyes, thinking he wasn't going to answer. But then he did.

"Gross?" He frowned. "I'm not sure that's the word I'd use. I suppose some people might say that sometimes it can be…unpleasant or upsetting. If someone dies in a violent way or in an accident, like Oren's parents did, there can be a lot of injury to the body."

"Were..." I cleared my throat. "Um...were Oren's parents really messed up?"

He sighed and leaned forward, resting his forearms on the desk. "I'll be honest with you, Evie. It was difficult."

"Difficult because it was gross?"

He stared at me for a long moment before he said, "Difficult because you never want to see people injured. Because it was a violent death. Because they were young and taken too soon. And a young boy was left behind. Difficult because the whole time I was thinking about how you and your brother would manage if something like that happened to your mother and me."

He was looking at me so intently that I dropped my eyes.

"It's not something I like to think about," he continued, his voice soft. "I have a job to do, but I'm still human and I have feelings. Sometimes the job is very hard."

I wasn't sure what to say.

Dad kept talking. "There are many reasons why it can be difficult. I see death nearly every day, but that doesn't mean it doesn't affect me. But that's not a bad thing. Empathy—the ability to understand other people's grief—is an important part of this job. Maybe the most important. The other stuff—the paperwork, dealing with the cemetery, arranging travel—it's just process. Caring for people is what really matters."

I nodded and looked down at my hands.

"Did Oren ask about his parents specifically?"

"No," I said, looking up and shaking my head. "No. *I* was just curious. I mean, he was *in* the accident, so he probably saw..." I was overcome with a wave of horror, imagining what he must have seen.

"He may have," Dad said gently, frowning. "But hopefully he didn't see too much or doesn't remember. The brain can do a great kindness during times of shock. Oftentimes people who are in catastrophic accidents end up with big gaps in their memory. No kid should have to remember something like that."

"I hope he doesn't remember either," I said. Then, after a long minute, I added, "His uncle wants him to go to therapy."

Dad nodded. "Probably not a bad idea."

"He doesn't want to," I said. "And it's not like he's super chatty, so what would he talk about?"

Dad smiled a little. "There's nothing wrong with him getting help. I hope someday he feels ready to receive it."

"Me too."

"But you're doing a good thing right now just by being his friend."

I looked down at my hands. "We're not really friends."

"Oh?"

I shrugged. "I mean, he's cool, it's just...I'm more of a loner."

Dad was quiet so long that I had to look up. "You?" he finally said. "A loner?"

"Yeah," I said. "I—that's how I like it."

He gave me a puzzled look before he said, "That doesn't really sound like you. Want to talk about that, Evie?"

I thought about Sam. My heart started to pound. I wouldn't have been able to speak even if I'd wanted to. I shook my head.

"Okaaaay," Dad said. "Well, whatever that's about, I can see that you're helping Oren, and I'm sure he appreciates it, even if you're not 'friends.'" He did air quotes around the word.

I cleared my throat. "I don't feel like I'm helping him very much."

"You are," Dad said. "Just give him time."

I rolled my eyes. "Everyone keeps saying that!"

"Because it's good advice." Dad smiled. "He seems to be enjoying your crafty stuff."

"It's art therapy," I said. "He's going to make a memorial for his parents out of the programs from their funeral."

"Really?" Dad tilted his head. "Was this your idea?"

"No," I said. "Well, the quilling was, but creating a memorial was his. He liked my picture and wants to make a tree of life using the programs."

He smiled. "That'll be perfect."

"Did you know that the name Oren means 'tree'?"

"I did," he said with a smile. "It's Hebrew. Just like your name in Hebrew means 'life.' And Natan means 'He gave.'"

"He gave *what*?" I asked. "He gave me a pain in the butt? Sounds about right."

"God gave us the blessing of a son," Dad corrected, pretending to be stern, but he was smiling. "We chose Hebrew names for you kids as a reminder of where we come from. Plus, Evelyn was your grandmother's name."

"I know." It was kind of weird to be named after a grandmother who had died before I was even born. But also kind of nice at the same time. Like I had a responsibility to carry on a tradition.

"I love the memorial idea," Dad said. "It's very fitting. I think you're right that it'll be therapeutic for him. I hope it makes him feel better to put that together. I'm looking forward to seeing it when it's done."

"I'll probably need to help him," I said. "Since he's a beginner quiller *and* he has his hand in a cast. But that's okay. I don't mind."

"Well, if anyone can help him, it's you," Dad said before he pushed back from his desk and stood up. "Now, it's getting late and I have a bit more work to do here before I can pack up for the night. Why don't you head home?"

"I'm not done yet though," I said, sliding out of my chair.

"Everything's fine," he said. "Go on home. Oh, and Evie?"

I looked over my shoulder. "Yeah?"

"The funeral is tomorrow morning. How do you feel about that movie in the afternoon? I could use a break."

"That would be awesome," I said. "I'm pretty sure Oren will think so too."

Twenty-One

Mrs. Eisen's funeral was scheduled for 11:00 a.m.

When I came downstairs for breakfast, Mom said they would make do without me and that I should stay home with Oren. But she said to be sure to wake up my brother in half an hour and tell him to get his butt next door by ten fifteen.

I would have been okay working, even if it meant leaving Oren by himself in our basement to watch TV or something—I wasn't his babysitter. My parents must have thought Oren would be upset if I left him by himself so I could work at the funeral home.

It wasn't like we could hide it from him though. All he had to do was look out a window and he'd see all the cars. He might even see them loading Mrs. Eisen's casket into the hearse.

I was tempted to tell my parents that he'd even been inside the building the day before because he wanted to learn more about funerals. But I was worried that then

I'd have to answer a ton of questions and maybe even get in trouble.

When Oren arrived, I told him about the movie that afternoon as I began to unpack my quilling supplies.

He pulled out his phone.

Why aren't you helping with the funeral?

"Nate will be doing everything today. He won't do as good a job as I do, but that's because he doesn't care as much. He doesn't want to be a funeral director when he grows up."

You want to do that?

I nodded. "Yeah. I mean, I'll have to go to school and everything, but I definitely want to be a funeral director. I'm already a junior funeral director." Sort of.

Oren looked impressed, which made me feel good.

"Anyway, we can work on this stuff until lunch. Are you excited about going to the movies?"

He shrugged.

I'd looked up what was playing, but I had no idea what kind of movies he liked. "What do you want to see? Do you like action movies? Superhero stuff?"

Another shrug, although this one also came with a small nod.

It was hard making all the conversation, even if I was getting pretty good at reading him.

He reached into my craft caddy for one of my fine-point markers. I thought he was going to start writing on some of the strips, or maybe scribble me a note, but instead he shoved the marker deep into the cast on his right forearm.

He jammed the marker in and out as he grimaced.

"What are you doing?"

Then the grimace turned to relief.

Ah, now I knew. I'd seen that expression on my brother's face the previous summer, when he had *his* cast. "Are you scratching your arm?"

Oren nodded and blew out a loud breath as he put the marker down.

"Can I sign it?" I said.

He blinked at me.

"Your cast, I mean."

He blinked again, and I started to fidget as I realized my mistake. Why would I want to sign his cast when I'd proclaimed we weren't friends? That we'd *never* be friends?

I looked down at the pile of paper strips in front of me and started to separate them into piles by color. "Unless you're keeping it clean on purpose. Or saving it for your actual friends or something. Ha ha. Forget I even asked. It's no big deal. Never mind."

Out of the corner of my eye, I saw Oren push back from the table. He got up, and for a split second I panicked, worried he was going to leave. "Wait, I—" I stopped talking because he was pulling his chair closer to mine.

He sat back down and placed his cast on the table in front of me with a thud.

"You want me to sign it?" I asked, a little breathless all of a sudden.

He nodded.

I looked down at the long cylinder of plaster. It was a bit dingy, but way cleaner than Nate's had been. I'd done a good job of helping Oren keep it clean. By the time Nate had his taken off, it was filthy and gross and smelled *so* bad.

What will I even write? I wondered as I tried to find the best spot on the cast. I didn't want to mess it up. Especially since I would be the first.

"Do you want your friends to sign it? Maybe they'll want to pick their own spots."

My old friends are weird around me now.

He was pretty good with the one-handed texting, I have to say. "They probably don't know what to say," I said. "Probably next time you visit, they'll be better."

He shrugged.

I don't want to visit. Everything back home reminds me.

"Of your parents?"

His head dropped until his chin was tucked into his chest.

So many things came into my head that I wanted to say. I wanted to tell him it would be okay. But I remembered Mom saying to just be there for him. And anyway, how could I tell him it would be okay? His parents were dead. He was an orphan. It would *never* be okay.

Mom was right. All I could do was be there for him, even if it didn't feel like enough.

"It's okay to cry," I said. "You don't have to be embarrassed. Crying is natural when you've lost...when you've been through hard stuff."

He sniffled.

"Do you need a hug?" I asked softly and then held my breath, worried that offering one hadn't been the right thing to do. But if it were me, I would want a hug.

Without lifting his head, Oren nodded again.

I got off my chair and closed the gap between us. Careful of his cast, I put my arms around him. I rubbed his back the way my mom did to me when I was sick or needed comforting. I didn't know if it was what he needed, but it had always helped me, and it wasn't like he was pushing me away, so I kept doing it. I didn't know what to say, so I did the hardest thing—I said nothing.

Finally he moved back and I let him go. I told him I'd be back in a second and left to grab the box of tissues from the bathroom. When I returned, I tugged a few out and handed them to him. "Feel better?"

He took a deep breath and dabbed at his face before he nodded. Then he lifted his damp and red-rimmed eyes to mine and nodded at me. I knew he was thanking me.

Before it got weird, I reached for my quilling tool. "Want to start on your tree?"

He handed me the marker and then pointed it at his cast.

Oh. I looked down at it again. What would I write? "I want to figure out the perfect thing," I said. "Let me think on it."

He lifted an eyebrow but nodded.

We got to work.

We started with the tree trunk. I suggested we frame it with the dark brown strips. Then we could fill it in with the pieces we'd cut out of the programs with his parents' names on them, alternated with more brown and beige so it would look like ridges in the bark. He liked that idea, but I wanted to get it just right, so I arranged everything first, pinning each piece into place before we got out the glue.

He handed me the strips and I placed them carefully as I chattered on about stuff. Lots of stuff. Paper quilling, my favorite types of paper, movies, archery, school—whatever I happened to think of at each moment.

He didn't seem to mind my talking. I even asked him once if he did and he smiled and shook his head. It was a lot of work to think of topics, but the more I talked, the easier it got. I just rambled about whatever.

And he listened. Not just pretended to listen, but *really* listened.

When we finished the trunk and I was about to get the glue, I noticed the leftover strips from the program. Many were from the edges and were mostly blank. I could use them for other things. But some were ones with his name on them.

"We should put these in," I said, pointing at the tree trunk. "So your name is in here too."

He shook his head fervently.

"Why not? They're *your* parents. You should be in the memorial picture."

He reached for his phone, but his fingers were still for a long moment as he stared at the screen. I was about to prod him when he started typing.

Finally he turned it toward me.

I am the tree. They are inside me.

My breath caught. I looked up at him, and his eyes were so serious. Like, he seemed really mature and wise. Even as he stared into my eyes, he pointed at his chest. Right at his heart.

"They *are* inside you," I said. "Forever."

He nodded.

"That's..." I had to take a breath before continuing. "That's really awesome and beautiful. I bet they're out there somewhere and are so proud of you."

He swallowed and then tapped at his phone again.

I thought ghosts aren't a thing.

Oh. I bit my lip as I thought about that for a second. I had said that to him, but at the same time...

"I don't think they are," I said. "Not like in the movies. But I think after people die, they are around us in some ways."

He lifted an eyebrow and then returned to his phone.

Like ghosts.

I laughed and rolled my eyes. "Not exactly. I mean, not around us like they can see us picking our noses or sneaking cookies. But maybe they're around us through our memories and the things we do." I pointed at the project in front of us. Then I placed my palm over my breastbone. "And in our hearts."

He smiled as he wiped away a tear.

For once, I'd said the exact right thing.

Twenty-Two

After a morning of crafting, we stopped to make lunch. Oren did most of the food prep while I set the table and made lemonade. We made a great team—working together like we'd been doing it for years. Better even than Nate and I, and we really *had* been doing it for years!

When everything was ready, we sat at the table and waited for everyone to come home. By then I was telling Oren about the finger sandwiches I'd eaten at my aunt's baby shower. My favorite ones were the peanut butter pinwheels wrapped around a banana slice. I was about to say I liked the egg salad and the ones with hazelnut spread almost as much when I heard the side door open. All three of my family members kicked off their shoes and came up the stairs.

"Lunch is ready!" I announced.

Mom smiled and shrugged out of her suit jacket. "Wonderful! What are we having?"

"Oren and I made a big salad and lemonade—nothing too fancy," I said, even though I was proud, pointing toward the table set with five places and the giant salad made of tuna, hard-boiled eggs, croutons and, of course, tons of veggies with ranch dressing. We'd even put out some of the nice napkins.

"This looks delicious, kids. Thank you," Dad said as he put a hand on my shoulder and gave me a squeeze. "But I have some bad news."

I glanced at Oren and then back at my father. "Was there another...I mean, do you have to do another—"

"No," he said as he went over to the kitchen sink to wash his hands. "Ecto is making some funny noises. I need to get her looked at this afternoon."

"Oh," I said. There was no use asking if Mom could take the hearse to the mechanic's. Ecto is like Dad's third kid and, like the very concerned parent he is, he always takes it—I mean *her*—in himself when there is something wrong that he can't fix.

I already knew Mom had an appointment at the hair salon, so there was no point asking her to take us. "So no movie, I guess?"

"Not for me, I'm afraid," Dad said as he sat down. "Maybe your brother could take you?"

"No can do," Nate said as he dropped onto his chair. "I've already got plans."

"Of course you do," I said. "Playing video games in someone's basement, I bet."

"Actually," Nate said, looking smug, "I'm helping out at the STEM camp. They're building robots and needed a hand."

"Oh," I said, feeling a bit sheepish. Robots weren't *my* thing, but I had to admit that sounded kind of awesome.

"That's wonderful, Nate," Mom said, reaching for the salad. "How did you get involved in that?"

Nate explained how his friend is a counselor at the camp and had asked him if he wanted to volunteer since he is such a computer whiz. It was the first thing I'd seen him get excited about in a long time. Maybe all those hours holed up in the basement and at his computer weren't a total waste after all. My nerdy brother seemed almost...cool. Huh.

When we were done eating, we took our dishes to the sink so Dad could load them in the dishwasher. "No reason you two can't still go see a movie," he said. "I can drop you off at the mall on my way to the mechanic."

"Cool," I said. Oren and I shared a smile. "Although we're very sorry you can't come with us!" I added quickly.

Oren nodded.

"Well, that makes me feel better," Dad said, laughing.

"I mean, come on," I said, reaching into his back pocket where he keeps his wallet. "Who will pay if you don't go?"

"You have a job!" Dad said, angling out of my reach.

"Movies are *sooooo* expensive though."

Mom snorted as Dad rolled his eyes.

"Fine, fine, movie's on me." He pointed at the table. "Finish clearing up first."

I grabbed the jar of pickles. "What about popcorn?"

Dad let out a dramatic sigh. "Fine. I'll spring for tickets *and* popcorn."

I grinned over at Oren. He looked pretty happy as he tossed back the last of his lemonade.

Even though it would have been fun if Dad had come, maybe it was going to be even more fun with just the two of us. Just a couple of—well, not friends, obviously. Just a couple of kids going to see a movie together, that's all.

I didn't really clue in until it was time to leave that Dad was going to drive us to the mall in Ecto—the hearse.

"Uh, Dad?" I said as he reached for the big silver door handle. "Are you sure we should…?" I nodded toward Oren. He was kind of gawking at the long vintage Cadillac.

"Oh, jeez. Yeah, guess you're right," he said. "Let's take the car. I'll swing back here and swap out before I go to the mechanic."

Oren shook his head and pointed at Ecto.

Dad frowned. "You *want* to go in this?"

Oren nodded eagerly.

Dad seemed pleased that Oren was so keen. "I did most of the restoration myself," he said as he opened the driver's door. "I'm not a mechanic, but I've learned a lot about this girl."

I opened the passenger door and waved for Oren to slide in. Since he was so interested, he could sit next to

Dad in the middle of the big bench seat. Dad talked about the car all the way to the mall.

I was glad I didn't have to pretend to be interested. I looked out the window, just happy that we were going out and doing something fun. I didn't even care what movie Oren picked.

I mean, I like quilling, but working on Oren's memorial picture that morning had felt...heavy. It was turning out really well—maybe the best project I'd ever done—but there was a kind of sadness hanging over it. I was glad to take a break from it. You can only think about sad things so much before you get really down. I learned that last year.

Dad pulled right up to the theater doors and stopped the car. "Have fun, you two. Oh, right, today's on me," he said, smiling at Oren as he handed me the money. "Text me when the movie's over and I'll come and get you."

Once we got inside, we stared up at the big board. "What do you want to see?" I asked Oren. There were several starting at around the same time.

He shrugged.

"I guess the superhero one is fine," I said. It wasn't my first choice, but, like I said, I was just happy to be there.

I bought the tickets and we lined up for snacks. I did a little math in my head. "If we share a big popcorn, we can each get our own drink." Oren agreed. Good thing, because he picked orange soda, which I think is the worst.

We took our snacks to theater six and chose seats near the back. He sat on the right of me so he could use his left hand for the popcorn. That way he wouldn't get butter all over his cast. Because we got lots of butter.

Thinking about his cast reminded me that I still hadn't figured out what to write on it.

Whatever it was, I wanted it to be meaningful. But everything I tried in my head sounded goofy. Even when the trailers ended, I was *still* thinking about it. So far? Nothing.

Sheesh, he'd be getting that cast taken off before I'd figured it out.

"That was so good!" I said as the lights came on nearly two hours later. I hadn't expected to like the movie so much, but it had been exciting. We were on the edges of our seats the whole time. I could tell Oren had liked it too.

I texted Dad as we made our way out to the lobby. He replied that he was on his way. And that's when I heard her voice.

"Oh look, Miri, it's *Evil*, the Corpse Girl!"

No, no, no, no. My back stiffened, but I kept on walking. I hoped Oren hadn't heard.

"Oh, Cooooorpse Girl," Sasha said in a singsong.

There was no way he missed that.

I looped my arm through Oren's good one, tugging him along as I sped up. "Let's go," I urged.

"Who's that with her?" I heard Miri ask.

"I've never seen him before," Sasha said.

"Don't ignore us, *Evil*!" Miri yelled so loudly that *no one* could possibly ignore her.

Still, I was planning on doing just that, but then the two of them somehow got in front of us, looking smug and…ugh, *so mean*. Miri had her hands on her hips, her feet spread wide. Sasha's arms were crossed.

Miri turned to Oren. "And who are you?" she asked sweetly. Sickly sweet, in fact.

"None of your business!" I snapped when Oren didn't answer. Not that I expected him to.

Miri looked at me. "I'm sure the new guy can speak for himself."

Uh, no, he can't, as a matter of fact. I tried to steer Oren away, but they kept blocking us.

"What do you think you're doing, Corpse Girl?" Miri asked. "Maybe the new guy wants to come hang out with us."

I glanced over at Oren. Did he? Would he rather hang out with the popular girls who might *want* to be his friends?

Oren shook his head. *Whew.*

"Oh, I get it," Sasha said. "He's your corpse boyfriend. I mean, look at his face, Miri! She probably dug him up at the graveyard."

Miri laughed like it was the funniest thing ever. Oren looked shocked. His hand went up to touch the jagged scar on his cheek.

I wanted to tell them what he'd been through so they'd stop. But I didn't want to embarrass him.

"Shut up!" I said. "You can be mean to me, if you want to so bad, but leave him alone!"

It wasn't until I saw their faces that I realized I'd yelled my words. I glanced over at Oren. He was looking at the floor.

"Aw," Sasha said, using that singsong voice again. "That is so cute. Corpse Girl is protecting her zombie boyfriend."

I snuck a peek at the faded bruises on Oren's face. I'd gotten so used to his injuries that I didn't even notice them anymore. He'd gotten the stitches out a few days earlier, but the skin still looked pink and tender.

"He's not my boyfriend!" I said. Oren looked a bit... something. Wait. Did he think...?

"I mean, not that you're not, I mean...we're not even friends...just...ugh!" I was so embarrassed. Now Oren probably thought that I thought he was not boyfriend-worthy. Not that I wanted a boyfriend. But that didn't mean the girls...ugh! I couldn't think straight.

Sasha and Miri laughed. "Oh no?" Sasha said. "Maybe he *wants* to be your boyfriend, Evil. Maybe he *likes* the smell of rotting flesh." She leaned toward me and sniffed loudly before she fake-gagged, her eyes rolling back.

Oren gasped.

Both girls looked at him. His eyes narrowed, and now he looked really, really mad.

So mad that I actually thought he might say something. He didn't.

"What's wrong?" Miri taunted. "Nothing to say, Zombie Boy?"

"SHUT UP! SHUT UP! *SHUT! UUUUUUPPPPP!*" I hollered. I couldn't have helped myself even if I'd wanted to. "You are horrible human beings! You have no idea about anything. You're so awful I wish you were dead!"

It worked. Both girls clamped their mouths closed as their eyes widened in surprise.

I glanced over at Oren. He was staring at me, tears in his eyes now.

He reached for his phone. For what? Was he planning a snappy text comeback? Too late for that!

"Come on," I barked at him. "Let's go. Dad will be here any second."

We stepped out into the sunshine.

You've got to be kidding me.

There was Dad, parked right out front. In the hearse. For all to see.

Pretending to ignore the snickering behind us, I grabbed Oren's good wrist and tugged him toward the car. I yanked the door open and dove in. Oren was right behind me, but he struggled to shut the door with his cast.

Which meant we both got to hear Sasha's parting words.

"There go the zombies. Back to the graveyard in their deathmobile."

Twenty-Three

"Did you have a good time?" Dad asked as Oren finally got the door closed.

"Fine," was all I could get out without bursting into tears.

"That's it?" Dad said as he pulled away from the curb. "Just fine?"

"Yes," I said, looking straight out the front window. "Perfectly fine. The movie was fine, the popcorn was fine. Everything's fine."

I could feel Dad's eyes on me, but I didn't dare look at him.

"Okaaaaay," he said.

That one word pushed me over the edge. "I mean, seriously, Dad? Did you have to pick us up in *this*?" I demanded. "Couldn't you pick us up in our regular car like a normal parent?"

Even though my face was trained on the road straight ahead, I could feel Dad's eyes on me.

"*Excuse me?*" he said.

"It's embarrassing!" I added, even though I could tell by his tone that I was on thin ice.

Dad squeezed his fingers on the wheel and then loosened them. "I'm sorry you feel that way, Evie. I'm not sure why it would be embarrassing to you all of a sudden."

"All of a sudden? Are you kidding?"

I heard him take a slow, deliberate breath.

"No, I'm not kidding," he said. Then he added a very stern: "And watch your tone please, young lady."

I huffed and bit my lip, keeping my words inside.

He'd never understand anyway. What did he know about what it was like to be me?

I glanced at Oren, but he was looking out the passenger window.

"Evie?" Dad said, sounding a little less stern now. "You want to tell me what happened?"

"No, thanks." We were almost home. I just wanted to put the whole thing behind me.

"Evie, I—" Dad began.

I sighed. "Dad, the movie was fine and we're good. Thank you for giving us the money. A couple of kids from school were laughing about the hearse, that's all. But I don't want to talk about it. Please and thank you."

"Oh," he said. Since I was practically mashed up

against him, I felt him deflate a little. "Well, I am sorry about that."

"It's fine," I said, working hard not to sound snarky. But which part of "I don't want to talk about it" did he not get?

Maybe he did get it though, because we drove the rest of the way home in silence.

I led Oren down to the basement and thought about leaving him there. I just wanted to go up to my room and be by myself for a while.

But as mad as I was, I couldn't abandon him. I kept thinking about how the girls had called him Zombie Boy. I knew how it felt. And it was my fault.

So I decided to stay with him until his uncle picked him up. I turned on the TV and started flicking through the channels. My phone pinged, but I ignored it.

Oren huffed.

I ignored him too.

He poked me in the arm and then aimed his phone at me, showing me the text he'd just sent.

Why did you let them get to you?

I looked from his screen up to his face. "Are you serious?"

He nodded.

"Because they tell *everyone at school* those things."

He shrugged.

So what? You don't want any friends anyway!

I stared at him. He stared at me.

I looked away first. "They called me Corpse Girl," I said quietly.

You should have stood up for yourself if it bothers you.

That made me mad. Really mad.

"I didn't see *you* standing up for yourself, Oren. *Or* me. You know, that might have been nice. For you to stand up for me and tell them that I *don't* smell like death or rotting flesh! That I'm *not* a Corpse Girl!"

He recoiled.

I wasn't done either. "Thanks for nothing. Though I bet if you'd *texted* them something, they would have backed down for sure."

He looked horrified. But I was still mad. My heart was pounding so hard. My mouth went dry even as my eyes started to fill with tears.

He shook his head.

"Yes you can speak!" I said, answering what he hadn't said. The tears were rolling down my cheeks now. "You just don't want to."

He frowned.

"I know you could if you wanted to," I said, crossing my arms. "But why won't you? Is it because you want everyone to keep feeling sorry for you because your parents died? Why?"

He started to cry then, his face crumpling in agony. My heart lurched as I was overcome with guilt. I'd gone too far. Way too far.

"Oren, I—"

"I killed them, okay?" he yelled. "I killed my parents. *That's* why!"

Before I could open my mouth, he was off the couch and running up the steps.

The screen door clattered shut behind him.

Twenty-Four

Had I heard wrong?

I must have.

But no. Nothing else sounds like *I killed my parents*.

It wasn't possible though. Oren hadn't killed his parents.

Had he?

No, they had all been in a car accident. One *he'd* been hurt in too. He still had the scar on his face, the cast on his arm, and I'd seen the bruises. I'd also seen his parents' obituaries, which mentioned the accident. He couldn't be making that up.

Unless he and his uncle were hiding something. But if he'd done something bad, wouldn't he be in jail? It didn't make sense.

I wanted to ask him, but he was long gone. And while his uncle's place wasn't far from ours, I couldn't remember exactly where it was, so I couldn't go find him. I got out my phone and opened up our texts.

My thumb hovered over the letters as I read his last message. **You should have stood up for yourself if it bothers you.**

I sighed and put my phone away. I picked up the remote and resumed flicking through channels. I needed time to think.

A little while later the doorbell rang. Assuming it was Oren, I muted the TV and waited. The ceiling above me squeaked as Dad crossed the floor to answer it.

When I heard *two* deep voices, I hurried to the bottom of the stairs to listen better.

Then Dad hollered down the stairs, "Oren! Your uncle's here."

I went up to the front hall where the two men stood. "Oren's not here," I told them. "He went home already."

Jared frowned. "I just stopped in to change so I could take him out for dinner. He wasn't there."

My heart fluttered in panic. Where would he have gone? "Oh," I said, looking out the front window, half expecting him to be out there on the street. He wasn't.

Just then the house phone rang.

"One second," Dad said as he hurried to grab it in the kitchen.

"When did Oren leave?" Jared asked me as he pulled out his cell.

"Not long ago." I reached for my own phone. But there

was nothing new from Oren. "Like, twenty minutes?"

Dad returned a minute later, a deep frown on his face. "Mystery solved. That was Sarah," he said. He looked at Jared to explain. "One of our cemetery groundskeepers. She said a very upset boy showed up at the Katzman graves a few minutes ago."

Jared's shoulders drooped as he sighed. "Thanks. I'll go get him." He turned toward the door.

"Wait," I blurted out before he could leave.

He stopped.

"Did Oren…" I cleared my throat. I was so scared to ask, but I had to know. "Um. He didn't, I mean, did…"

Jared turned fully toward me now, eyebrows high on his forehead as he waited for my question.

"Evie," Dad said. "What's going on?"

I exhaled. "Did he…did Oren…he didn't kill his parents, did he?"

Dad roared, "EVIE!"

Jared added an equally shocked, "WHAT?"

Sudden tears pricked at my eyes. "I'm sorry, I'm sorry! I just—"

Jared looked at my father and then back to me. "Of course he didn't!" he said.

"Why would you even ask that?" Dad demanded.

I hurried to explain. "Because he told me he did."

Both men stood there gaping at me.

Jared finally spoke first. "What do you mean, he *told* you? He's speaking?"

"Just the one time...um...he was pretty upset and..."
I cleared my throat again. "He said he...killed them."

"That's ridiculous," Jared said. "It was an *accident*.
Why would he say that?"

"I don't know," I said, suddenly worried I was about
to get in trouble. "He just...blurted it out. Like, for no
reason."

Jared sighed and sat down on the bench by the door,
dropping his head into his hands. He spoke as he rubbed
at his face. "I just don't know what to do. He lost his
parents, and now he's stuck with an uncle he barely
knows who doesn't have a clue what he's doing. He's
uncommunicative. He's having nightmares. He won't go
to counseling." He muttered a few curse words and then
said, "I'm making such a mess of all this. I don't know how
to be a parent. I don't know how to be what he needs."

"He has been doing art therapy," I said.

Jared looked up at me. "What?"

"We've been doing crafts. I think it's helping." At least,
I had *thought* it was helping. Now I wasn't so sure.

"Oh." Jared gave me a sad smile. "That's...that's great,
Evie. Really. If it weren't for you,"—he looked up at Dad—
"*all* of you—I'm not sure what I'd do."

He sighed and then continued, "I was at their house
earlier, getting the mail from the neighbor and figuring
out some bills. I'm going to need to sell it sooner or later
so we can wrap up the estate. Anyway, I found a folder."
He paused and shook his head.

I glanced at Dad, but he gave me a look that said this was one of those times when listening was way more important than talking.

Jared took another breath and went on. "They were planning to take Oren to the Grand Canyon a couple of weeks from now. I was actually thinking of taking him— no one needs a holiday more than he does. But...instead I called the travel agent and canceled everything. I just can't..."

"You have so much on your plate," Dad said, laying a hand on Jared's arm. "You can take him another time. He'll understand."

Jared gave him a grateful smile, but the feeling wasn't in his eyes. "I don't think he knew they were taking him."

He looked so miserable and hopeless, it broke my heart. Actually, broke it *more* because it was already pretty busted over Oren. "I'll go get him," I offered. I felt like I should, since I'd been the one to push him into freaking out and running away.

"I should go," Jared said. But he didn't move.

"No," I said. "I want to. And...uh...I might owe him an apology."

"Does this have something to do with what happened at the movies?" Dad asked.

"Um, maybe? Sort of," I admitted. This was not the time to get into it. "Anyway, I'll go. It's not far. You two can stay here."

Jared nodded.

"Come on in," Dad said to him. "I'll put on a pot of coffee." He led Jared toward the kitchen while I went down the five stairs to the side door.

I had one sandal on when I heard Dad say my name.

"Yeah?"

"Call if you need a pickup," he said, adding, "Don't worry. I'll bring the car."

I smiled up at him. "Thanks, Dad."

Twenty-Five

I jogged most of the way to the cemetery. When I got to the parking lot, I had to stop for a moment to catch my breath.

I saw Sarah standing at her front window. The curtains were pulled back and tucked behind her. When she noticed me, she pointed out at the cemetery.

I gave her a little wave and started toward Oren, who was sitting on the grass beside his parents' graves. The sod and dirt hadn't quite settled yet, so there were still two low humps where they were buried. Sarah and Richard watered the new grass often, so it might even be wet and squishy. I hoped Oren hadn't found that out the hard way.

I picked up two smooth oval stones at the edge of the parking lot and tucked them into my palm. I walked slowly toward him, trying to figure out what to say.

There weren't any headstones marking his parents' graves yet—there wouldn't be for a while. There wasn't a big rush. Dad had told me once that Jewish custom says you have a whole year to put them in.

When the headstones were ready to be placed, there would be another small ceremony, called an unveiling. Friends and family would come, the rabbi would say a few prayers, people would place little rocks on top of the headstones, and then everyone would go to someone's house to eat lunch.

When I got closer to Oren, even though he was looking down at the ground, I could see that his face was blotchy. It didn't seem he was still crying though.

"Hey," I said softly.

Startled, he looked up. When he saw it was me, his eyes went back down to his hands.

"Mind if I sit with you?"

He shrugged.

Thankfully, the grass was dry.

Some people might think it's weird to sit in a cemetery, but I don't. Maybe because I've been here a million times. It is quiet and weirdly peaceful. Some people walk their dogs down the paths like it's a regular park. And, of course, some people come to the cemetery to visit the ones they've lost.

One lady—Mom said her name is Mrs. Carlin—comes every week and sits on a bench next to her husband's grave. She pulls her knitting out of her purse and just sits and knits for an hour or two.

I've wondered if she used to sit next to her husband on their sofa and knit him sweaters or scarves when he was alive. I bet she did. When she visits, she doesn't cry or even seem like she is mourning. It's like she just wants to be close to him. I think that's nice, though I do wonder who she's knitting for now.

I've even seen people talking to graves. I've never gotten close enough to hear what they are saying, not wanting to disturb them, but maybe they were telling stories about their lives now. Maybe they were praying.

As I snuck a glance at Oren, I thought that maybe some people even ask for forgiveness.

I cleared my throat. "Oren?"

He didn't speak, but I knew he was listening. "Your uncle is at my house. He..." I took a deep breath and figured I'd just get it out there. "*He* says you *didn't* kill your parents."

Oren's head snapped up, and he glared at me. He was clearly not happy with my sharing that with his uncle.

"He said it was an accident."

Oren returned his eyes to the ground and yanked at a few blades of grass. I hoped Richard wasn't watching—he took his grass very seriously.

"Are you saying it *wasn't* an accident, Oren?"

He shook his head slowly.

What did that even mean?

"Can you please explain it to me?" I said, trying very hard to be patient. "Because it doesn't make any sense."

This time he didn't even shake his head—he just ignored me.

"Were you driving?" I asked.

He snorted, but that was all the response I got.

"Oren, come on." I leaned into his shoulder.

Nothing.

"Have you told *anyone* what happened?"

That got me a head shake. Not that I was surprised. I knew about keeping big secrets.

But this was something Oren needed to deal with. His uncle had no idea. And he'd said Oren wouldn't go to therapy. He needed to talk to *someone*.

Putting the rocks I'd collected down on the grass, I reached for his hand. I slid my fingers in between his and gave him a reassuring squeeze.

"Can you tell *me*?"

He pulled his fingers away.

I tried not to take it personally, even though it was hard not to. "I won't tell anyone. I promise."

He sighed and got out his phone. I wanted so badly for him to *talk* to me. It was tempting to make him mad again so he would, but then he'd just run away. And I didn't really want to upset him again.

I looked out at the cemetery as he typed. Richard was raking the grass a few rows away. It was almost like he was raking a regular lawn, if you could look past the headstones and the fact that there were dead people in the ground under all that grass.

Finally Oren nudged my shoulder with his as he turned the phone toward me.

No.

"No?" I said. All that time to type two little letters? "What does that mean?"

His eyebrow went up.

I rolled my eyes. "I know what *no* means. But I'm asking—" I sighed. "Never mind. You're not going to tell me, are you?"

He shook his head.

"Ever?"

That got me a shrug.

Did that mean maybe?

"Fine," I said. "Whatever. The real reason I'm here is to tell you I'm sorry I was mean to you after the movie. It wasn't fair. I guess I was mad at those horrible girls and took it out on you. I didn't mean to."

Before I even knew what was happening, I was crying again. Big, fat tears falling down my face.

Oren leaned into me, which felt good but for some reason just made me cry more.

"They're so awful," I said. "I mean, I'm sorry, I shouldn't be crying because you're here and your parents are dead and your life is way worse than mine, but they're just... ugh...you must think I'm the most horrible person ever, and I—" I stopped talking because I was just making it worse.

When I braved a look at him, he was staring at me. Waiting.

"I am the worst. Sometimes I speak before I think. I don't mean to. It just happens."

He started typing.

I know that. It's OK. Those girls are awful.

It meant a lot that he thought so too. "Right?"

I wiped at my eyes.

DYNAH?

"Dynah?" I said, confused. "Those girls were Miri and Sasha. Who is Dynah?"

He rolled his eyes and returned to his phone.

Do You Need A Hug? DYNAH

"Oh!" I laughed. Then I nodded and leaned toward him. He put his good arm around me and patted my back.

"Thank you," I said a minute later as I pulled away from him. "You forgive me, right?"

He made a "hmm" face and looked up at the sky like he was thinking about it.

"Oren!"

He smiled and then nodded.

"Dork," I teased.

He picked up my round stones and looked at me.

I was happy to change the subject. "It's Jewish tradition that when you go to someone's grave, you place a stone down." I pointed at the shiny black headstone next to his parents' graves. "Look there at Mr. and Mrs. Adams. See all the little rocks piled on top of their headstone? That means a lot of people have visited. They were old, so they probably have a lot of kids and grandkids who come to pay their respects."

He looked at my rocks again.

On the other side of his parents' graves was a single headstone that read *Hannah Menkowitz*. I did the math in my head. She was forty-four when she died. No mention of her being a wife or mother. There were no little rocks on her headstone. How sad.

I got up onto my knees and placed the stones on the new mounds of turf. "One for each of them," I said to Oren. "I want to mark that I was here."

Oren jumped up, and for a second I thought he was going to run away again. But he went over to the parking lot and picked up several stones. He returned and carefully laid one on each of his parents' graves too.

Then he leaned over and put one on Ms. Menkowitz's headstone. Then another on the Adamses', which was really nice.

He looked...not exactly happy. But maybe a bit less sad.

"We should get back," I said. "I'm sure your uncle's worried. Maybe you should let him know we're on our way."

As we passed the house, I gave Sarah a little thumbs-up, since she was still peeking out her window.

"He's a good guy," I said to Oren. "Your uncle, I mean. He's really worried about you, you know."

Oren nodded.

"He thinks he's doing a bad job as your guardian. He wants to help you, but he's pretty new at this parenting thing. And I guess with your not talking and not wanting to go to therapy, he's sort of—"

"We were fighting," Oren said suddenly.

The sound of his voice shocked me so much I stopped in my tracks. Both that he'd spoken and what he'd said. His voice was different this time. He sounded like a regular kid, which shouldn't have surprised me, but it kind of did. I tried to act like it was no big deal.

"Who was fighting?" I asked. "You and your uncle?"

"No." Oren shook his head and sighed as we started walking again. "Me and my parents. In the car that day."

"Oh," I said.

"I was in the back seat, and we were going to the grocery store. It was just a regular day, you know?"

I nodded and bit my lip, not wanting to say anything that would make him stop talking. If ever there was a time that I did not want to talk someone's ear off, it was right then.

"We were talking about the rest of the summer. I was so mad that they wouldn't let me go to wilderness camp. All my friends were going, and I've never been camping and had been really looking forward to it. I couldn't understand why they didn't want me to go."

So *that* was why he'd seemed weird about camping. I felt bad for ever bringing it up, but how could I have known? Then I thought about what Jared had said about the Grand Canyon trip—was that why they wouldn't let him go to wilderness camp? Because they had a huge surprise trip planned?

"I freaked out. I…I was just so mad." He sniffed a couple of times and then continued. "I told them I hated them."

"Oh no, Oren." I slid my arm across his shoulders as we walked.

"It gets worse." He swallowed loudly. "I told them…" His voice was barely more than a whisper. "I told them I wished they were dead. Then I'd be able to go to camp."

I gasped. I hadn't meant to—it just slipped out.

We'd stopped walking and Oren was crying really hard now, his hands, even the one in the cast, covering his eyes. I felt tears on my own cheeks too.

I grabbed the sleeve of his T-shirt and tugged on it. "You didn't make the accident happen, Oren," I said. "You *didn't*! We all say things we don't really mean. Trust me, I know."

His eyes were squeezed shut as he wiped his tears away. He hiccupped and tried to take a breath, hiccupped again, inhaled and then spoke. "But that was the *last thing* I said to them! The accident happened right after that!"

I felt him start to tug away from my grasp. I held on harder. I couldn't let him run away. "No," I said sternly. I yanked his shirt until he opened his eyes and looked at me. "It. Was. An. Accident."

I thought about my mom and how good she was with grieving people. When I'd asked her how she did it, she said to just be calm. Listen. Figure out what the person needs from you. Whatever it might be.

Right now Oren needed more than anything to understand that he wasn't responsible for his parents' deaths. "I get that you feel guilty," I said, keeping my voice steady. "And I know how it can seem like it must be something you did. That you made it happen."

"But I *did*. I told them—"

I held up my hand. "You didn't mean it. You didn't *really* want them dead, did you?"

"Of course not!" He seemed shocked at the question.

"Were they good parents?"

"The best!" he squeaked out. "I just didn't understand why they didn't want me to go to wilderness camp. I was so angry."

"Okay, so here's a question," I said. "Don't you think that *the best* parents would know you didn't really mean stuff you blurted out when you were mad? *My* parents always do."

I'd had more than my share of blurty temper tantrums. But Mom and Dad would just roll their eyes and send me to my room until I calmed down.

"I really didn't mean it," Oren said, his bottom lip twitching.

"I know," I said, looking into his eyes so it was clear I really meant it. "And they did too. They *knew* that. They *knew* you loved them more than anything!"

He stared at me, the tears pouring out of him, his chest rising and falling as he breathed hard.

"They knew," I said again. "I'm 1,000 percent sure of it."

As he looked at me, something in his eyes changed.

He tugged his shirt away from my fingers, but this time it was so he could wipe his eyes with his sleeve. As I did the same thing, I realized something.

"That's why you stopped talking, isn't it?" I asked. "Because of what you thought your words made happen."

He didn't answer. He didn't have to.

"I completely understand," I said, channeling my mom again. I took a deep breath while I put together what I wanted to say in my head. This was not a time for rambling. "But Oren, words can be good too. Like every time your parents told you they loved you. Or that they were proud of you. Or when they told you stories that made you laugh. Or when you made *them* laugh. Right?"

He nodded. "I guess so." In a very soft voice he added, "But...Evie?"

"Yeah?"

"It was the last thing I said to them before...before it happened. I can't ever change that."

There was so much anguish in his voice that it made my heart ache.

"No," I agreed. "You can't change that. But if the accident hadn't happened, you would have apologized, and they would have forgiven you, right? It would have been no big deal, just a random argument where you said something you regretted."

"I guess."

I stopped on the sidewalk and faced him. "So tell

yourself that they *did* forgive you—they just didn't have a chance to say it in person."

He looked over my shoulder as he shrugged.

"Oren," I said, getting right in his face to stare in his eyes again. "They loved you, they forgave you. They probably didn't take you seriously at all. They knew you were upset."

After a long minute his face scrunched up. "It still hurts, Evie. It hurts so much."

"I know," I said, trying to keep it together for him. "It'll probably always hurt, but maybe not as much? My dad says you never stop missing someone who's died, but the pain gets less..." I struggled to remember how he'd described it. "Sharp? It probably doesn't seem like it now. But it will get better." I realized that I was also talking to myself. And that my dad was absolutely right.

He sighed. "But..."

"What?"

"Does it stop hurting because I have to start forgetting about them?" he asked, his lip quivering. "Because I don't want to forget them."

"No," I said. "You will *never* forget them. But you will start to remember the good parts about them more than the bad."

He swallowed. "I don't think I can forget about the accident."

"No," I said. "Probably not. But maybe you'll think about it less."

After we walked for a few minutes without speaking,

Oren said, "You know, Evie, you're pretty smart about this stuff. You've learned a lot from your parents."

"Thanks," I said. "I have learned from them, but…"

He looked at me. "But what?"

Maybe it was time to tell him the truth about Sam.

"Evie?"

I sighed. "But I lost someone once. Not someone in my family like you did or anything. But I was friends with a kid at camp last summer. His name was Sam."

"Wait," Oren said. "I remember you mentioned him. I thought you got in a fight. You said there was drama."

"Not fight drama," I said. "*Death* drama."

"Was he in an accident?" Oren asked softly.

I shook my head. "No, he got sick. One day I went to arts and crafts to meet him, but he was gone. He'd had to go to the hospital and then…" I shrugged.

"Oh, Evie," Oren said. "That's really sad. Did you go to the funeral?"

I shook my head. "No. He lived in a different city, and I didn't find out until later. I…I made him a get-well card and sent it to his home. But…his mom wrote me a letter back to tell me that he'd gotten worse and then…" I took a deep breath. "You know."

"I'm sorry," Oren said.

"After that…" I sighed. "I sort of freaked out. Started obsessing about dying and what happens… you know, after. It was really scary, but not knowing felt worse, so I get why you want to know. It's why I started studying what happens at funerals and paying attention, wanting to learn exactly what my parents do and how they make it better for people." I cringed. "I mean, as better as it can be when you've lost someone important."

"What did they say when you told them about Sam?"

"I never told them."

"What?" Oren frowned. "But that makes no sense. Your parents are so great and—"

"I know, and it seems silly now," I admitted. "But at the time...I don't know. It just felt overwhelming and private, you know? I can't really explain it."

"Wait." Oren blinked at me a few times like he was trying to work something out. "Is that why you're"—he did air quotes—"a 'loner' who 'doesn't want friends'?"

I shrugged.

"Evie," he said. "Did you really think you could avoid getting sad ever again by having no friends for the rest of your life?"

I glared at him and then looked down at my sandals. "I don't know. Maybe."

"You can't just decide not to have friends," he said.

I snorted. "Uh, yes I can. And I did."

He laughed, drawing my eyes up to his face.

"What?"

"Evie, that's the most ridiculous thing I've ever heard."

What? Did he really just say that? I started to walk away from him.

"Evie, wait!" He grabbed my arm, stopping me. "Hold up. I don't think *you're* ridiculous, but… okay, here's a question. What do you think *we* are?"

"Huh?"

He rolled his eyes. "Uh, I hate to break it to you, Evelyn Walman, but we're friends. You and me."

I shook my head. "No we're not."

"Call it what you want," he said, grinning even though his face was still red and blotchy. "But we are totally friends."

"Shut up," I said, but I didn't mean it. Why was my heart pounding so hard?

"Maybe even *best* friends," he said with a wink.

"Nuh-uh!" I said, trying not to smile now. "Okay, fine, yes, it seems silly now. But we really had fun. And when I found out what happened to him…well, it really hurt."

Oren nodded. "I understand. But…" He tilted his head.

"What?" I asked.

"*We* could have fun, you know."

I blew a loud raspberry and rolled my eyes. "Okay, whatever, fine. Let's be"—I did air quotes—"*friends.*"

He leaned into me. "Deal."

"So, *friend,*" I said. "DYNAH or what?"

"Yes," he said. "Especially if it makes you stop talking for, like, five seconds."

I smacked his arm. "You never *complained* about my talking!"

"I wouldn't have gotten a word in edgewise if I'd wanted to!" He laughed, and then his face got serious. "I actually like your talking, Evie."

"Really?"

"Yeah," he said seriously. "And what you said before about words being good? *You* are how I know that's true. You are a good friend, even if you don't want to admit that quite yet."

"Really?" I squeaked out, a sudden lump in my throat.

He nodded. "The best."

"Well, good luck getting me to shut up now!" I said as I threw my arms around him for a hug that maybe I needed as much as he did.

Twenty-Six

When we got to my place, I led Oren inside the side door and listened. The voices I heard were low, but I could tell they were all upstairs in the living room.

"Why don't you go wash your face?" I suggested to Oren.

He nodded and kicked off his sneakers before he started toward the bathroom.

I went the other way into the living room. All three of them, Mom, Dad and Jared, stared at me.

I glanced over my shoulder to make sure Oren wasn't behind me before I said, "He'll be here in a second. I apologized, and we're good."

"He's okay?" Jared asked, and then added, "I mean, as okay as he can be?"

"I...I think so. But, um..." I stumbled, not sure what to say.

Then I didn't have to say anything, because Jared's eyes moved to behind me.

He stood up. "Oren?"

Half a second later Oren rushed past me and threw himself into his uncle's arms.

He was crying, but I heard him mutter, "I'm sorry, I'm sorry," over and over into his uncle's shirt. And then he added a warbly, "I love you." Mom and Dad looked at me, shocked to hear Oren speaking.

Jared's face crumpled as he held Oren tight. Like he never wanted to let him go. It was exactly what Oren needed too. He clung to his uncle like his life depended on it. Maybe it did.

When the sobs subsided, he held Oren away and looked down at him. "You *do not* have to apologize, Oren. You have absolutely nothing to be sorry for. *I'm* sorry that I haven't been what you need. I just hope that..." He trailed off as he started to really lose it too.

Oren hiccupped and took a bunch of breaths, trying to calm himself. It was funny how now that he wanted to talk, he couldn't.

"Evie," my dad said, his hand on my shoulder. I wasn't even sure when he'd stood up—I'd been so focused on my friend and his uncle. "Let's go get started on dinner."

My parents and I quietly left the room, leaving Oren and his uncle to talk.

Once we were in the kitchen, Mom and Dad basically cornered me between the fridge and the cupboards.

The only escape would have been into the broom closet behind me.

"What happened?" Dad asked softly.

"Nothing," I said with a shrug. "We just sort of talked some stuff out."

"He's speaking now?" Mom asked, flicking her eyes toward the living room.

"I guess so." I didn't want to tell them what he'd told me about the accident because it was private. Maybe he'd tell his uncle, but that was up to him.

Mom and Dad tried to stare it out of me until I began to fidget. "What are we having for dinner?" I asked, trying to change the subject.

"I've barely given it any thought," Dad said and then looked at Mom. "Thai?"

Mom nodded. "Great idea. We can see if Oren and Jared want to join us."

"That sounds nice," I said.

Mom pulled me into a hug. "I don't know what you did to help Oren today, but whatever it was, thank you."

It made my heart happy to hear her say that. Not just because it felt nice to be thanked by my mom, but because even though Oren and his uncle were in the other room crying and were still really sad about Oren's parents, at least Oren was talking now. I'd upset him at first, but I'd been there for him, given him what he needed.

I thought of something else he needed. And how maybe I could make it happen.

"So I have an idea," I said to my parents. "What if…"
I let them in on my plan.

They loved it and said they'd talk to Jared about it.

I just hoped he was on board.

Twenty-Seven

The next day it was rainy, so Oren's uncle dropped him off on his way to work. Oren told me he hadn't had time to have breakfast, so I asked Mom to make us a giant cheese omelet to share.

While we ate, my parents got ready for work. They returned in their non-funeral clothes, which meant no services today. Then they filled their coffee mugs and went next door, promising they'd be home for lunch.

Oren and I went into the dining room, where I had all my quilling stuff set up so we could work on his tree memorial.

"François!" I scolded. The cat was perched on the table, chewing on a strip of paper. Oren tugged the paper away, scooped the cat up and put him in his lap, stroking him with his good hand. A moment later the cat settled and began to rumble in pleasure.

I started making more leaves to add to the pile in front of me. Big leaves, small leaves, dark green leaves, light green leaves, medium green leaves. So. Many. Leaves. Did I mention quilled trees require *a lot* of little coiled leaves that take forever to make? It's relaxing but also kind of boring after a while. At least I had someone to chat to.

Make that chat *with*, now that Oren was talking again.

As I worked on the millionth leaf, Oren studied what we'd already pieced together. So far it was just trunk and branches—we'd arrange all the leaves perfectly before I started gluing them in place.

"Hmm," he said.

"What's wrong?"

"It needs something," he said.

"Well, yeah." I rolled my eyes. "*Leaves.* Working on it." I pointed at the giant pile of coiled paper leaves in front of me.

"No," he said. "Something *more.* Hmm. Like…how about roots? Yeah. Roots." He reached over to the pile of strips left over from the funeral programs and started separating some out.

I leaned over but couldn't tell what he was doing. "What are those?"

He looked at me. "My grandparents' names. They should be in the roots, because they're part of my family too."

"That's a really smart idea," I said. "I like it."

"Yeah," he said a bit wistfully.

"Do you see them a lot?" I asked, adding, "Your grandparents, I mean."

"Not really." He shrugged. "My mom's parents are in Israel with my other uncle. They send really nice packages of stuff for my birthday and visit sometimes, but I don't know them that well. They invited me to move in with them," he added, "but I didn't want to go that far away. Plus, Uncle Jared's here."

"What about your other grandparents?" I asked. "Your dad's parents?"

"They're older and live in a retirement home now. When I was a lot younger, they used to take me to the fair. My grandpa and I would share a big plate of funnel cake and then we'd go on the rides. One time I barfed up the funnel cake after we went on the teacups. All over my grandma's shoes."

"Oren!"

"I know." He laughed. "My grandmother *still* complains about how she had to throw those shoes out because she couldn't get the greasy barf off them."

"So gross!"

"I visit them sometimes. But not very much since…" His voice trailed off, but he didn't need to finish his sentence.

Dropping my eyes, I smoothed a strip of paper between my fingers as the silence stretched between us.

"Anyway," he finally said. "I like my uncle. He's trying really hard. And yesterday made it…better. It's just…" He sighed.

"He's not your parents," I said.

He nodded.

"I get it," I said. "But he loves you. He really wants to be a good uncle for you."

"I know," he said. "Last night after dinner he showed me pictures of him and my mom and my other uncle from when they were kids. It was weird, but also kind of nice. It helped me remember her from before the…from before."

I smiled as I finished up the leaf I was working on.

"He still wants me to do to therapy," Oren said several minutes later as he arranged a few more piles of strips for the roots.

"Would it be so terrible?" I asked honestly. I've never been to therapy, but I know that a lot of people who lose loved ones go. My parents even keep brochures for grief counseling in a holder in their office in case anyone wants them. "My mom always says it's a good way to sort out your feelings. It's just talking. She was going to be a therapist before she worked next door. It's just normal people talking about normal things."

He shook his head. "I think it *would* be terrible. I just…I don't know. I think it would make things worse. I don't want to talk about it."

I wasn't sure if he meant he didn't want to talk about going to therapy or he didn't want to go to therapy to talk about his parents. Whatever he meant, I didn't want to push him, so I left it at that.

We worked away in silence, and for, like, the first time ever, I didn't feel I had to talk. Just being with him was all I needed right then. Maybe that's what he needed too.

Was this what being best friends was really like? I wondered. If so, I was okay with the quiet.

Eventually Oren broke the silence. "Hey, Evie?" His eyes were down as he fiddled with the papers.

"Yeah?"

"Are you ever going to sign my cast?"

I glanced at the still-unmarked cast on his right arm. "I don't know what to write," I admitted.

"You?" he asked as he gawked at me, eyebrows raised high on his forehead. "*You* don't know what to say?"

I rolled my eyes. "It's different. Whatever I write on your cast will be there forever."

"Well, not forever," he said. "I'll get it off eventually." The face he made told me "eventually" was not soon enough.

"Still. Everyone will see it. I don't want to write something I'll regret. Or worse, that makes *you* regret we're friends."

"Evie," he said.

"All right!" I reached for my pencil case and pulled out a fine-tip green marker. Then I thought better of it and traded it for a thick brown one. Brown? No. Nobody wants brown writing on their cast. I traded the brown for purple as I thought about what to write. What had Nate's friends written on *his* cast? Mostly silly stuff that didn't make sense to anyone but him. Inside jokes, I guess.

"Are you stalling?" Oren asked.

"Yes," I admitted. "But we don't have any inside jokes yet."

"What?"

"My brother's friends signed his cast with random inside jokes. But we don't have any."

"Do you not *want* to sign it?"

"I do!" I said. "I just...let me think about it some more, okay?"

"Fine," he huffed and then turned his gaze to the picture again. "I think we should fill in the sky with blue. Maybe some curly white clouds too."

"All right," I said. "But I'll need to cut some more blue strips. I don't have any ready."

"I wish I could help more," he said, holding up his cast. "You're doing most of the work. And...I think..." He looked more closely at the picture.

"What?" I asked.

"I want you in it too."

I blinked at him as he pointed down at the picture.

"Maybe like...a bird? Or the sun? A rabbit maybe? Something special that's separate from the tree but represents you."

I didn't know what to say. "Oren, no...I...I shouldn't be in it. This is for your family."

He shook his head as he looked at me seriously. "I want you in the picture. I want to be able to look at this and see you in it because you are my friend and you helped me." Did he mean that I helped with the picture or that I helped *him*?

Maybe both.

"Okay," I said. "If you're sure. A bird would be cool. What kind?"

He gave me a smile. "I'll leave it up to you what kind of bird you want to be. But when you figure it out, write your name on some of the strips you use to make it. Like I did with the programs."

"I'll think about it," I said. It was a bit overwhelming, the idea that he'd want me in his picture. "But for now, pass me that folder. I'll have to cut a bunch of blue for the sky."

He handed me several sheets of different shades of blue as I pulled my paper cutter toward me. I started to cut the paper, one long strip at a time.

He made a face. "Isn't there an easier way to do that?"

"You can buy ready-made strips," I said. "But I use different kinds of paper to give my projects texture. See, like, the trunk?" I pointed at the picture. "We used all those different types of paper for the programs, but the precut strips you can buy especially for quilling are all the same boring paper."

"Makes sense," Oren said. "But I wonder...could you use a paper shredder to make them? Just, you know, feed the paper in and zip, zip, zip, you've got strips."

I had never thought of that! "That's a great idea," I said. "My parents have one in the office next door."

"Can we go?"

He hadn't mentioned wanting to go back to the funeral

home since that time we'd snuck in. "You sure you want to?"

"Yeah." He shrugged. "We're just going to shred paper, right?"

"Right," I said, pushing back from the table.

"But Evie?"

His tone made me freeze. "Yeah?"

"I still want to see...you know...the other *stuff* there."

I understood what he was saying, but we probably couldn't manage it today, even if I'd wanted to—my parents were there.

"Okay," I said. "Let's go."

Twenty-Eight

"Oh."

Oren and I were in the funeral home office, staring into the bin I'd just pulled out of the bottom of the shredding machine.

"So that didn't work," Oren said.

"Thanks, Captain Obvious," I said, using one of my dad's favorite sayings. I dug my hand into the blue confetti. Pretty blue confetti, but it wasn't strips. It was definitely confetti.

"What's going on?" Dad asked as he came into the office.

"Uh, we thought the shredder would make strips we could use for quilling." I held up a handful of the tiny paper pieces to show him.

"Oh." Dad chuckled. "It was a good idea. You know, if it weren't a crosscut shredder."

"Thanks, Captain Obvious!" I said.

"Wait. I thought *I* was Captain Obvious!" Oren said. "So. What now?"

"Well," I said, "unfortunately, that was all the blue paper I had. So how do you feel about going to the stationery store?"

It was still raining, so Dad said he'd drive us after lunch. But by then the sun was out, so Oren and I decided to walk. The air was muggy and smelled like worms. We even had to avoid squashing them on the sidewalk. But it felt good to be outside.

When we got to the stationery store, I introduced Oren to Suzanna. It felt so weird that she had no idea his parents had just died. He told me later that it was a relief, for once, not to see that "look" people usually gave him when they saw him.

It made me think a lot about grieving people. How sometimes they were devastated and heartsick, but other times they could seem like everything was fine. Like, how no one would know that underneath the smile Oren was *really* hurting. Sort of like how I'd been after I'd found out about Sam. How I sometimes *still* felt when I thought about him or opened up my memory box and sorted through his origami paper.

I took Oren over to the racks and racks of different kinds of paper. I showed him my favorites, describing what I liked best about each. He actually seemed interested, which was nice. When I talk to my parents about paper, their eyes quickly glaze over.

"There's so many!" Oren exclaimed.

"I know. Do you want to pick some that look good to

you? Remember, you'll be seeing most of them on their edges."

He glanced over the papers and then, for some reason, his cheeks got all pink.

"What's wrong?"

"I...I don't have a lot of money," he said. "My uncle gave me a little in case we go for ice cream or something, but probably not enough for paper. I didn't know we were coming here today."

"Oh, that's okay," I said, waving it off like it was no big deal. "I've got money from my job at the funeral home."

"But..." He looked uncomfortable. "I've already used lots of your supplies, and it was my idea to put the paper in the shredder. I want to buy you more." He shoved his hand into the pocket of his shorts and pulled out a five-dollar bill. The crumpled little flowers I'd made him were folded up in it.

"Oh," I said, pretending I hadn't seen the flowers, though secretly I loved that he still carried them around everywhere. "Five dollars is a good start. I usually buy paper one sheet at a time." I pointed at the little price stickers on the racks. "See? They're all individually priced, depending on the type."

"Perfect," he said. "We can buy enough to get started and then come back later to get some more."

We pooled our money and bought twenty-eight sheets of different types and colors. It was more than enough to finish his memorial and replace what we'd already used. Paper goes a long way when you cut it into strips.

We thanked Suzanna and left the shop. And, because it's just my luck, who did we see but Miri and Sasha.

My heart started pounding as I glanced at Oren. He rolled his eyes.

"I knew I smelled something rotten," Sasha said, a look of disgust on her face. She really had that look perfected. Lots of practice, I guess.

I tried to walk past them, but Miri stepped in front of us. "Well, well, well, if it isn't Corpse Girl and Zombie Boy."

"Get out of our way," Oren said.

"Oh look, Miri," Sasha said. "Zombies *can* talk after all."

"Careful he doesn't eat your brain, Sasha," Miri said in a pretend whisper.

Oren snorted. "You'd have to *have* brains for me to eat them," he said. "I guess I'd starve around you two."

I laughed.

Sasha sputtered.

Miri narrowed her eyes. "You think you're so smart?"

Oren shrugged. "Smarter than a couple of girls whose best insult is telling someone they're a zombie. Please. Everyone knows zombies are awesome." He put his arms straight out, widened his eyes and started moaning.

I giggled. I'd never seen him act so silly.

"She lives at a funeral home," Sasha pointed out, as though Oren didn't know.

"I live *next door* to a funeral home," I corrected.

Then, like a flash of lightning, I remembered what I'd seen on the funeral home website. And the something I now knew about Sasha's family.

"The funeral home," I added, "where *your* grandmother went to when she died."

"What? No way," said Sasha.

"That's right. Her name was Sandria Kepler, and she died eleven years ago. My parents took care of her."

Sasha didn't say anything but swallowed hard.

"What did you do to her grandmother?" Miri demanded. "You didn't..."

"You're kidding, right?" I said. "You really aren't very bright, are you? I was a baby then, just like you were. But my parents treat every person who comes into our funeral home with respect. They don't eat brains, they don't make fun of people, they don't do anything other than what is exactly right." I spoke calmly and with authority, feeling a sense of pride for my parents' profession.

As the girls stared at me, their mouths hanging open, Oren jumped in, breaking out of his zombie character. "Evie's parents are amazing—supporting the families of the people who have died too." Then he narrowed his eyes and added, "Even if their grandchildren are selfish jerks. So maybe you should think twice about picking on Evie for what her family does. Someday you're going to need them. Think about *that*."

"Oh, and you know what else, Sasha?" I blurted out, even though it hadn't seemed like Oren was done talking. But I was on a roll now. "Your grandfather? He helps out at our funeral home too. He's part of the chevra kadisha, the special team that prepares bodies for burial."

Sasha laughed. "He does not. *No way* he would ever do anything gross like that!" she said.

"Oh no?" I crossed my arms and stared straight into her eyes. "Maybe you should ask him. How do you think he knows my parents so well? You remember the ice cream shop?"

I would have kept going, but Miri grabbed Sasha's wrist and dragged her into the store, the bell on the door tinkling as it closed behind them.

I took a deep breath. "So that was fun," I said.

Oren snorted. "Is that true about her grandfather?"

I nodded. "Yeah," I said and then turned toward him. "What about you? Did you mean all that? About my family?"

"Seriously?" He did a double take. "You have to ask?"

I shrugged. "I guess not, but it's nice to hear. What else were you going to say?"

"That you smell nice. Like strawberries."

"Aw, thanks!" I said.

He nudged me with his shoulder. "Come on. Let's go finish this project."

But we didn't have a chance to get back to it, because as soon we got in the house, I knew there had been a death.

Mom came down the stairs in one of her charcoal-gray suits. "Oh, good, you're back," she said. "Can you run next door and do a quick tidy? I have a family coming in a couple of hours. I didn't think we'd have anyone until after Shabbat, but..." She shrugged. "Your father and I need to go to the hospice."

Then she seemed to notice Oren standing beside me. "You're welcome to hang out downstairs until Evie's done," she said to him.

He glanced at me and then back at Mom. "I'm good at dusting and vacuuming. Is it okay if I help?"

She blinked, obviously surprised. "Oh...uh...are you sure?"

Oren nodded. "You don't even have to pay me or anything."

"Thank you. If you want to help, you're welcome to." Mom reached forward to ruffle his hair a little. Oren seemed to like it. I wondered if his own mom used to do that.

Once she was gone, Oren asked, "Will there be anyone else in there?"

"Probably not." I looked out the window at the parking lot. "Syd's car isn't there."

"Let's go," Oren said. "I'll help you clean, and then you can show me some more stuff."

I'd already suspected this was his plan when he volunteered. "How much do you want to see?"

He thought about that. "I don't know. Can I decide as we go?"

I nodded. "Sounds good. All right, let's go."

We got next door just as my parents were pulling away in Ecto. We waved at them and then went around to the side door. I pressed the numbers on the keypad to open the door.

"They'll be gone for a while, but I don't know how long. Want to look at stuff first?"

Oren bit his lip.

"I can't show you a dead person," I said. "There aren't any here. And even when there is one, someone is always here watching over them. So if you really want to see one, it's going to be complicated."

"What do you mean 'watching over them'?" Oren asked, frowning.

"Remember when I told you how the soul sticks around until the funeral?" When he nodded, I explained, "A person has to sit with the body to say prayers and comforting things, so the soul feels better and isn't scared about... you know, what happened."

He stared at me. "Someone has to sit and comfort the ghost."

"Sort of. But it's not like movie ghosts," I reminded him.

He looked skeptical.

"My parents do shemira all the time, and they've never seen any ghosts," I assured him. "It's an old tradition to protect the person when they're vulnerable.

"Anyway," I said. "What I'm saying is, if you really want to see a body, it's going to be difficult."

"Okay. Let's start with that room where they..." He pointed at the door marked Private.

"All right," I said, leading him to the double doors. "You ready?"

He took two deep breaths.

"No. But let's do it anyway."

Twenty-Nine

"Wait!" Oren barked as I started to open the door.

I froze. "What?"

"You know what?" he said. "Let's go clean first. We promised your parents, and I don't want to run out of time."

Even though what he said made complete sense, I knew he was stalling. It was a little annoying that he kept changing his mind, but I understood. He wouldn't be able to unsee anything I showed him, so it was best if he was completely and totally sure.

We dusted, vacuumed and tidied up the office, making sure it was ready for my parents to meet with the family of whoever had died. I even filled up the holder of brochures for grief counseling. I did it *really* slowly, adding…one…yellow…brochure…at…a…time.

If Oren noticed—which I was hoping he had—he didn't say anything.

Finally everything was perfect and ready. I asked him if he wanted to go to the prep room. I even said it was fine if he had changed his mind and would rather not. We could always go back to the house and work on his memorial project.

But no, he wanted to see the room. Now he was ready.

This time he didn't stop me when I opened the doors. I flicked on the overhead light, which buzzed a little, making the room bright and almost blinding. The walls were stainless steel from the floor up to about halfway and then stark white to the ceiling. It felt clean and cold like a hospital room.

I tried to see everything like it was my first time too. The floors were speckled but smooth, made of the same stuff as the hallways at school. But in the middle of the floor there was a drain for cleaning. There were several cabinets around the room, holding supplies. There was a counter with a sink, like in a kitchen, but this one was for washing hands, not dishes.

In the center of the room was a big white table. It was sort of like an examination table you'd see at the doctor's office, but instead of being padded and covered with paper that sticks to your butt, it was ceramic, like a flat bathtub with ridges. It was tilted slightly and had a drain at the end that was positioned over a sink that hung on the wall.

I glanced over at Oren. He was staring at the table.

"That's where they wash the…people," I said softly, not wanting to freak him out more. "They even take off all their nail polish and makeup." I pointed at the cabinet above the counter. "There's nail polish remover and makeup wipes up there."

He looked at me but didn't say anything, so I cleared my throat and went on. "And when they wash them, they have to do it a special way, and in a particular order, pouring buckets of water over the person, washing each part of the body carefully while they say prayers. It's really respectful. Anyway, after they do the bucket thing, the water goes in there, obviously." I pointed at the sink.

Oren nodded.

"Then, after they wash them, they have to dress them."

Oren frowned. "Wait. What do they dress them in? Like, fancy clothes? No one asked for...I mean, I don't remember..."

It took me a second to figure out what he was talking about. "Oh, are you asking where they get the clothes they wear?"

He nodded, swallowing hard.

"On TV they show people wearing suits or their favorite dress. But it's different for Jewish burials." I walked over to the big cabinet in the corner and opened it up. Inside were several shroud kits, neatly stacked and wrapped in white plastic. They were marked for women or men and also by size. I pulled one off the stack on the right. *Women's Small.*

Oren came up beside me. "What is it? A nightgown?"

"No," I said. "It's called a tachrichim, or a shroud. It's like a special burial suit." Before I could think too hard about how I shouldn't, I carefully opened up the package and pulled out the items of clothing. They were made of thin, pure-white fabric—pants, a shirt, belts, a long overcoat, and head covering. No pockets, buttons, zippers or Velcro—Dad said the clothes were very traditional and had to be loosely tied with the plain belts that came in the package.

Oren slowly reached forward and touched the fabric. "So...this is what my mom's wearing?"

I nodded. "Yes. And your dad would have been dressed in something really similar, just the man's version."

"Okay," he said, though his voice was shaky. He was really struggling, and my heart hurt for him, but I was proud at the same time. He was facing a really big fear and was being so brave about it.

"It's like pajamas," I said. "At least...you know they're comfortable. I feel sorry for those people who get buried in suits. They have to spend all of eternity in uncomfortable clothes."

He blinked. "I guess."

"So that's pretty much it in here," I said, looking around. "It's a lot like a doctor's examination room."

He nodded. "It's...yeah, I guess I thought it would be a lot more...I don't know...like a lab?"

I shrugged. "Maybe at a non-Jewish funeral home. Where they use chemicals and do embalming. They sometimes even do makeup and hair for the deceased person. To make them look...I don't know, like they did when they were alive. Or less dead."

"Geesh."

"Yeah. For when they have open caskets for the funeral or viewings."

"I don't think I would have wanted to see that."

I nodded. "Me either. But Dad says some people find comfort in seeing their loved one that last time. To say goodbye, I guess."

"What about if they were..." Oren looked down, and I almost didn't hear when he said, "In an accident. Would they still put them on display?"

"I don't know what they do at other places. Maybe? I would think it would be up to the family," I said. "But it's not something we really have to worry about, since it's not allowed in our culture. I will have to learn more about it all when I go to funeral director's school though. Dad says you have to learn about everything—even the non-Jewish stuff like embalming and all that."

"There's a school for funeral directors?" he asked, surprised.

"Yeah. You have to go to school to get licensed. Kinda like a doctor, but for dead people."

"Huh," he said. "I guess I've never really thought about how you would learn all the stuff you need to know. But it's just like any other job—you need to get trained for it."

He looked around the room again and then back to me. "And this is what you want to do when you grow up?"

"Yes." I nodded. "And it's not because my parents are making me. After the whole thing with Sam, I realized there was so much I didn't know. Like, what happens to the person who died, or how the people left behind are supposed to move on."

Thinking about the time right after I'd found out about Sam was hard. I swallowed and quickly added, "But doing the research made me realize how important what my parents do is. How important it is that there are people trained and willing to do the really hard stuff."

"You'll be good at it, Evie," Oren said with a gentle smile. "I mean, you already *are*."

It was the best compliment ever. "Thank you."

I returned the shroud kit to the package and closed it up, sliding it into the center of the stack so no one would notice it had been disturbed. I didn't think I'd done anything wrong to it, but maybe Dad wouldn't love that I'd used it for show and tell. He hadn't brought one to career day at school, so maybe you weren't supposed to show people.

"Let's get out of here," I said and led Oren to the door, flicking the light off. When we got out in the hall, both of us let out loud breaths, like we'd been holding something in. Then we looked at each other and laughed.

"DYNAH?" I asked.

"Nah, I'm okay," he said. "Can we see the caskets though? Last time I was too nervous to take a proper look."

"Really?" I asked, surprised. "You sure?"

"Yeah," he said, looking not so sure. "I'm already freaked out, so may as well."

"All right." I took him to the front of the chapel and into the casket display room. I guess it's sort of morbid to other people to look at caskets, but to me, they're just furniture. Furniture that I have to dust all the time.

There were ten models lined up on carts so they could be moved around easily. They came in different styles and colors, but all of them were made from wood—no metal is allowed, not even nails—and were arranged from the fanciest shiny, dark ones at the front to the very plain, unpainted pine boxes at the back.

It reminded me of IKEA, where you can go and see a giant room filled with sofas. They all do the same thing—it's just up to you to decide which one you like best or can afford. Dad says it's traditional to have a very plain, modest casket because it's not supposed to be about luxury, but some people do like the fancier ones that are more expensive.

"Whoa," Oren said as I led him deeper into the room. Jared had picked out the matching caskets for Oren's parents on his own, which I'd thought was smart—Oren shouldn't have to deal with that. Even *I* might not be able to do that, and I was in here nearly every day.

"This one," he said, walking over to a shiny, honey-brown one in the middle of the room. Of course he'd remember. He'd had to stare at them all through the funeral service. Then he'd watched the two caskets get lowered into the ground.

He walked to it and ran his finger over the polished wood of the lid and traced the Star of David that was the only decoration on it.

I bit my lip to keep from talking too much. I could tell this was one of those moments where Oren needed quiet with his own thoughts.

Finally he looked at me. "Can I see inside?"

I nodded. Even though we don't ever have open caskets at funerals, most still have lids that are split in half, so you can open the part where the person's head and upper body are. Maybe the factory sells them to non-Jewish funeral homes too, and it's just easier to make them all like that.

I reached for the edge of the lid.

"Wait!" Oren said, his good hand coming to my wrist to stop me. "What am I going to see?"

"We don't keep people in them. Or mannequins or anything," I assured him. "It's just straw with a fabric covering."

"Straw?"

Easing out of his grasp, I pulled up the lid. All we could see was the thin white fabric lining. As I held up the lid with one hand, I pressed the lining on the bottom. It crinkled and felt lumpy and coarse underneath. "The straw is like bedding, a bit of padding so the person isn't lying right on the bottom."

Oren eyed the inside of the casket warily. But I could tell he was interested too.

"You can touch it," I said. "It's sort of like what's at the bottom of the hamster cage at school."

"Oh," he said. "Okay. That's...I guess I never thought about what goes inside. It's probably pretty dark in there when the lid's closed, huh?"

"I guess so," I said and then for no reason added, "It's not scary. Want me to get in?"

Oren's eyes went so wide. "You wouldn't."

I shrugged. "It's just a wooden box."

His face became a tumble of emotions, and I knew I'd gone too far. He was really freaked out now.

"I'm sorry! I was just trying to..." My breath caught as the guilt stuck in my throat. "I wanted to show you that it's not scary!" Except I'd just done the opposite.

"Can we...?" He exhaled loudly. "I think I've seen enough for today."

"DYNAH?" I asked.

He nodded, and I put my arms around him in a hug. When he pulled back, he had to wipe away a couple of tears.

"You okay?" I asked. I hoped I hadn't just given him reason for more nightmares.

He nodded. "Yeah. I think so. Thanks for showing me all this."

"Let's go back next door and work on the quilling," I suggested. "We've got some time before your uncle comes to get you."

"Okay," he said. "But…can…uh, I think I dropped something in the office. I'll just run and grab it."

Before I could ask what he might have dropped, he jogged back to the office. He only took a minute, so whatever it was, he'd found it quickly.

When I saw a bit of yellow poking out of his shorts pocket, I clued in.

I didn't mention the brochure, but I was really happy he'd grabbed one.

Thirty

On Monday morning I was in the kitchen, sitting at the table with my orange juice and peanut butter toast, looking forward to Oren's arrival. Even though the weekend had been jam-packed with family time, I had missed seeing him. I got that he was supposed to be spending time with his uncle and maybe even visiting his grandparents at the retirement home, but I wondered if he missed me too.

We were besties, after all.

I was just wondering what he and I would do for the day when I got a text from him.

Sick! Not coming today.

Oh no! What's wrong?

Barfed. Uncle Jared too. He's a bad cook.

😋 **What did he make?**

Burritos. Not bad going down. So gross coming up. Worse than funnel cake!

🤮 🤮 🤮

He sent a few more funny emojis and then said he was tired and going back to bed.

It turned out it was not food poisoning. Neither of them was better the next day, so they must have gotten some sort of flu. Mom and Dad said it was lucky I didn't get it, given how much time Oren and I had been spending together. I didn't feel so lucky and was still pretty grumpy about it because now I was stuck at home by myself. Bored out of my mind.

It helped a little that Oren checked in a few times a day. When he wasn't sleeping or barfing, I mean.

Mom even took over some matzo-ball soup for them that Dad had made from scratch. It was a nice thing for her to do, but it would have been nicer if she'd let me go with her to visit my friend.

I finished as much of Oren's memorial picture as I could. I had added myself too—in the form of a snowy owl sitting on one of the branches of the tree. I'd written my full name—Evelyn Marcia Walman—in black marker on some of the strips I used to make it. The ink peeked out and looked cool, just like feather markings. I couldn't wait for him to see it. I had something else to show him too.

It felt like forever before his uncle returned to work and Oren felt well enough to leave his house. By the time he showed up on Thursday morning, I was so desperate to see him I could barely stand it.

Finally he came walking down the street. I had been waiting for him and threw the door open the second he started up the porch stairs.

I was smiling so hard that my face hurt.

"Hey, Evie," he said. "It's been a while!"

"I know!" I said. "I'm glad you're feeling better."

He wasn't just *feeling* better either. He looked amazing. I hadn't realized how much I'd gotten used to his injuries after the accident. He still had his cast on, of course, but all traces of bruising were gone from his face and even the scar down his cheek had healed a lot—it was much lighter than it had been. And the circles under his eyes were gone.

"Come on in," I said, waving him inside. "I can't wait to show you how the picture is looking. I hope you don't mind I've been working on it."

"Not at all," he said as he followed me into the dining room.

"FRANÇOIS!" we yelled together at the cat hunched on the table, enjoying a strip of paper that was sticking out of my bin. Startled, he ran off, taking the paper with him.

"He's for sure going to barf that up somewhere," I said as I shook my head. But I was relieved the cat hadn't damaged the picture at all.

I held my breath as Oren stared at it. Until I couldn't hold it anymore. "So?" I asked, my heart pounding. "What do you think?"

He looked at me, his eyes shiny with tears. "Evie, I love it."

I exhaled in relief. "Even the owl?"

He nodded as he looked back at the picture. Then he held it up at arm's length. "Especially the owl. Seriously, it's perfect. So *you*. Wise and—"

"Hooty?" I finished for him.

He laughed. "Sure. Let's go with hooty. Seriously, though, I really love it. Thank you."

"I have something else," I said nervously. "Something I want to show you."

He put his picture down and nodded. "What is it?"

I took what I'd been working on out of the bin. It was another picture, this one of an origami crane, but instead of being made of folded papers, it was created out of dozens of small quilling shapes put together. Before I could say it, Oren said, "For Sam."

My throat got so tight, all I could do was nod.

"It's really nice, Evie."

I took a breath. "I made as much as I could out of the origami paper he gave me. I was saving it for...I don't know what, but this feels..."

"More meaningful," Oren finished. "He would have liked that, I think. You should frame it."

I nodded, so thankful that Oren got it. We got each other. That's what being friends means. And now that I'd accepted we were friends, I wouldn't have had it any other way.

I was about to thank him with a hug but suddenly the side door opened. Oren and I looked at each other. "Who's there?" I called out.

There was some stomping on the stairs and then Dad came around the corner. He was wearing a suit, but the tie was loose and messy. He looked exhausted.

"Dad?" I said. "I thought you were still in bed!"

He gave me a weak smile. "No, we got a call late last night."

Oh.

"Where's your mother?" he asked.

"Right here," Mom said, coming into the room. She was wearing capri pants and a pretty white-and-red checked shirt—normal everyday clothes. "I'm taking Nate to the orthodontist."

Dad's face fell in disappointment. "Syd's next door now, but he can't stay. I was hoping you could do a shift while I get some sleep."

"Sorry." Mom shook her head. "It took months to get this appointment."

"All right," Dad said. "I'll just grab a quick shower. Funeral's tomorrow morning at eleven. Graveside."

Mom nodded. "I'll send an email to the ladies to tell them tahara will be tonight at eight."

Dad turned to me and opened his mouth.

"Got it," I said. "Dusting, vacuuming—I know the drill." I turned to Oren. "Want to help?"

He nodded. "Sure."

"You're good kids," Dad said. "Remind me after I get some sleep to take you out for ice cream."

And then he shuffled off to take his shower.

Mom hollered at Nate to hurry while I packed up the quilling stuff so the cat wouldn't get at it.

Then Oren and I went next door.

"So," he said as we crossed the parking lot, "there's someone in there?" I knew he wasn't talking about Syd.

I nodded. "A woman, since Mom and her volunteers are doing the tahara later."

When he was really quiet, I could almost read his mind. I stopped walking. "Are you sure you want to see?" I'd so hoped that showing him everything else would squash his curiosity. Apparently not.

He shrugged. "Maybe?"

I started walking again. "If you see, you can't unsee, you know," I warned.

"I know," he said.

"Anyway," I said with a wave toward the black SUV near the side door, "Syd's in there, so…"

"Is he right in the same room?"

"I don't know. But we'll have to start with cleaning anyway," I said, buying some time.

We started in the chapel. I got out the polish and we worked on the pews until everything gleamed and the place smelled lemony fresh. I even got down on the floor to look for any stray tissues from the last funeral. There weren't any on the floor, but I did find one tucked into the corner of a pew. You have to check everywhere.

We were almost done when Dad came in. His hair was slightly damp and he had on a different suit. He still looked tired though. "Hey, kids," he said. "Looks and smells good in here—great job. Syd's off, but I'll be in the quiet room if you need anything."

"Thanks, Dad," I said.

Oren gave me a look after Dad had left, but I shook my head and returned to my work.

When we were done in the chapel, I went into the supply room to get paper towels. The supply room where the fridge is.

"Is she…" Oren whispered behind me, nearly scaring me out of my skin.

"Gah!" I exclaimed, whirling around to face him. "What are you doing?"

He nodded toward the giant stainless-steel fridge. "Is she in there?"

"I think so," I said, reaching for a package of paper towels. "But come on. We should fill up the holders in the bathrooms."

"I want to see," Oren said, determined.

"My dad is in the next room!" I whispered. "We can't!"

Just then I heard a noise. I tilted my head to listen.

I heard it again. It was my dad's super-loud snore coming from down the hall. Oren's eyebrows went up and he came fully into the room, the door closing behind him with a gentle *snick*. He went past me to go right up to the fridge door. "Come on."

I glanced toward the door to the hall, my heart beginning to race. "We shouldn't."

"Just a peek before your dad wakes up."

He put his hand on the fridge's big door handle.

"Wait!" I said, taking the few steps to stand beside him.

"What?" he said.

"You were scared to even look in the casket," I said. "What makes you think you're ready to see a real live... er... *dead* person?"

He opened his mouth. Then closed it. Then opened it again and said, "I don't know. I just want to."

"Because you didn't get to see your parents?" I asked softly.

He took a gaspy breath, like he hadn't expected my question and it had punched him in the gut. He swallowed hard. "Maybe."

"Do you think it will make you feel better? About them being gone, I mean?"

I watched as his face crumpled in slow motion. I didn't have to ask him if he needed a hug. I just threw my arms around him and held on tight while he cried. I patted his back and made shushing noises into his ear, but he just kept on crying for what felt like forever.

Finally he pulled away from me. I reached over to the storage rack, grabbed a packet of tissues and pulled two out—one for each of us.

"I'm sorry," I said.

He sniffled as he wiped his eyes. "I don't know how

I'm supposed to feel," he said. "One minute I'm with you and it's like life is normal again. But then I remember that they're dead and everything sucks. Then I feel guilty for ever having fun. Even just laughing. Because they're dead and they can't have fun anymore."

I nodded, my throat tight with emotion. I still managed to say, "They'd *want* you to have fun. They'd want you to be happy."

He looked down at the wet tissue in his hands. "It feels wrong though. Like I don't deserve it."

"Maybe..." I took a breath. "Maybe you should try to go to therapy. You know, just once?"

"Hey, my uncle told me this morning that your parents called and invited us to come on your camping trip."

Yes! Finally my parents had put my plan into action! Although...I stared at Oren for several blinks, trying to figure out what one thing had to do with the other. "That's great, but huh?"

He looked at me and a little smile turned up the corner of his mouth. "Sorry, that was random. He said you asked your parents to invite us because I didn't get to go to wilderness camp."

"Yeah," I said. "But what does that have to do with therapy?"

He twisted up his mouth. "He said we can go *if* I agree to go to therapy."

"Oh," I said, not saying out loud that I thought it was a good bargain. "So what does that mean?"

"It means he's totally bribing me," he said with a roll of his eyes. "But whatever. I really want to go camping."

"So…" I looked at him questioningly.

He shrugged and made a face. "I guess I'm going to therapy."

I gave him another hug because I was thrilled about *both* things.

"That is amazing, Oren! I'm so excited!"

He nodded. "We're getting our own campsite. Uncle Jared says we need some time to bond and get to know each other." He made a face, like he thought the bonding thing was a bit much, though I knew that deep down he probably wanted that too. "But we'll be near you, and we can do marshmallows and canoeing together."

"That is such good news, Oren," I said.

"I know, but…" He looked over my shoulder at the fridge again. "I…keep…keep thinking about what you said…that some people need closure by looking at the dead person in the casket?"

My heart sank. "Yeah?"

He pressed his lips together. "I think…I think I need that."

I grimaced. "Are you sure?"

He took a deep breath. "I think so."

"You can't just 'think so.' You need to be *sure* sure."

"I'm *sure* sure."

"Fine." I didn't love the idea, but he was determined. "Let's open the door together."

With a nod, he wrapped his good hand around the door handle right above mine.

"On three?" I said.

"On three," he agreed.

"One," we chanted together.

"Two."

"Thr—"

"WHAT ARE YOU TWO DOING?"

Thirty-One

I squeaked in surprise as Oren and I whirled around to face my dad. He was standing in the doorway, red-faced and looking madder than I'd ever seen him.

Oh no.

We both dropped our hands from the fridge door handle.

"I asked you a question!" he said in a much quieter voice, but he was still just as mad.

I burst into tears. I didn't mean to, but my dad *never* gets angry. Right now it looked as if steam was going to start shooting out of his ears like in one of those old cartoons.

"Follow me," he said very sternly. "Both of you." He turned and left the storage room. Oren and I looked at each other and then hurried to follow him down the short hall into the quiet room.

"Sit," he barked, pointing at the sofa that faced the door.

Oren and I lowered ourselves onto it. I wondered if he was as nervous as I was. Was his heart pounding as hard in *his* chest?

"Now," Dad said. "Tell me what you two were doing in there."

"Uh, we were—" I was about to lie, but I knew he'd lose his mind even more if I did. I was definitely in trouble already, I didn't want to be in trouble forever. I sighed and opened my mouth to tell him the truth. Oren beat me to it.

"I'm really sorry, Mr. Walman," he said. "Please don't be angry with Evie. I wanted to see...a body. I thought it would give me closure about my parents. I...I asked her to show me. It's all my fault."

Dad sighed and sat down on the couch across from us. Then he stood up and came over to ours. "Move over," he said. Oren and I both shifted, making room so he could sit between us.

He took a long breath before he started to speak. "Listen," he said, his voice now very calm. "I'm sorry I yelled. But you can't, under *any* circumstances, gawk at a deceased person to satisfy your own curiosity. It is not only incredibly disrespectful, but I don't think either of you are ready."

I exhaled in relief. Oren did too.

Dad snorted. "Clearly I was correct in that assumption."

He turned toward Oren. "I understand your wish for closure. What happened to your family is a terrible tragedy, except for one important thing."

Oren swiped at a tear with his thumb. Dad put his arm around him and pulled him close. "The one important thing is that you survived. I won't lie to you and tell you it's going to be easy for you—you know better anyway—but your parents are up there somewhere, and they are *so* thankful that you survived. As a parent I can tell you nothing would be worse than losing a child. *Nothing.* And they are so thankful and relieved that you made it out of that accident."

"I don't always feel that way," Oren whispered. "It hurts so much."

"I know," Dad replied sadly. "It will for a long time, but it *will* start to hurt less. And it may not seem like it's enough now, but you have an uncle who loves you very much and wants to do right by you." He glanced at me and smiled. "And you have friends who care about you a great deal. It *will* get easier. It may not seem like it will, but I promise you."

"Oren's going to go to therapy," I said.

"That's great to hear," Dad said as he gave Oren another squeeze. "I think you'll find it really helps."

Oren nodded and sniffled. I reached across my dad and handed him a tissue. "He's also coming camping," I said. "If…"

Both Dad and Oren looked at me.

"If we're still going, of course." I beamed my sweetest smile at my father.

"She shouldn't be punished, Mr. Walman. It *was* all my idea," Oren repeated. "I'm really sorry. I…I didn't realize how disrespectful it would be. I just…I wished

I could have seen my parents one last time before…" He pressed his lips together and shook his head.

Dad sighed. "I can't speak for your mother, since I didn't see her. If you really need to know, you can ask Evie's mom. But I can tell you that your dad was at peace. His injuries were mostly on the inside, and the coroner said it happened very quickly. I know that probably doesn't help, but it means he didn't suffer. There wouldn't have been anything anyone could have done. Including you."

He pulled Oren in tighter as I snuggled into Dad's other side. Oren hiccupped.

Dad went on in a soft voice. "A body often looks in death as it does in life—like a very still sleep. I think probably the thing I notice most is the pallor." He lifted his hand and touched his own cheek before he draped it around me and pulled me closer. "The blood stops moving through the veins, so the skin loses that pinkness we take for granted. Otherwise, like I said, they look asleep and at peace. Does that help?"

Oren nodded and took a deep breath. "Yeah."

"Good," Dad said.

Then we sat there for a long time. Just being together, thinking and dabbing at tears.

Finally the silence started to get weird.

Dad began to breathe really deeply. Then he began to snore softly.

I poked him in the side. "Dad?"

He gasped awake. "Sorry, sorry," he said, groggy. "Long night."

"So does that mean I'm not in trouble?" I asked.

He pretended to think about it and then shook his head when I poked him again. "No, I guess not. Because if you were, we wouldn't get to go for ice cream later. And banana splits are health food, right?"

I rolled my eyes. "You're such a dork," I said. "But I love you anyway."

"I know you do," Dad said, his eyes saying it too.

"Let's go, Oren," I said as I stood up. "I guess we have to finish cleaning up out there."

"If you're up for it," Dad said, looking at Oren.

"Yeah," Oren said. "I feel better. I—is it weird to say I kinda like it here?"

"Yes," Dad said with a chuckle. "But it means you fit in very well with the rest of us. Now go finish cleaning, and I'll see you two later this afternoon."

We left the room and went to the storage closet to get the vacuum. We both glanced at the fridge.

"You okay?" I asked.

Oren nodded. "I think so. I mean...I *will* be. A lot of that is thanks to you, Evie."

I shrugged. "What are junior funeral directors for?"

He shook his head. "I think you mean, 'What are *friends* for?'"

"Yeah," I said, grinning at him. "I guess that too."

This summer

Sitting on a log in front of a warm, crackling campfire, I used two chocolate-lined graham crackers to slide the perfectly toasted marshmallow off the stick.

When he'd pulled the ingredients out of the cooler, Dad had tried to convince us that this combination was his invention. He called them s'Bens, but I knew for sure that s'mores were invented even before Dad was born. And c'mon. *S'Bens*? That didn't even make sense!

"Here you go," I said as I handed the gooey mess to Oren. "Try not to get your cast all sticky."

"That won't be a problem," he said. "The entire thing is going straight into my mouth." And, as promised, he shoved the whole thing in. His cheeks bulged out like a chipmunk's. I laughed as he struggled to chew.

"How's it taste?"

"Gooth," he said, "Thankth!" Bits of graham cracker came flying at me.

"Gross!" I reached for the bag of marshmallows to toast one for myself. I'd already made a bunch for my parents and Jared, who were sitting on the other side of the campfire on their own log, talking about whatever. But after two each, they'd said no more, so now I was making them just for us. Nate wasn't a fan of marshmallows, so he was sitting off to the side, eating a bag of chips. My parents pretended not to notice that he was on his phone, texting.

"Speaking of my cast," Oren said once he'd swallowed. "I go to the doctor next week, and he might be taking it off." He looked so excited. I couldn't blame him for wanting to get rid of the itchy thing that kept him from doing fun things like quilling and swimming without a plastic bag taped on his arm.

His cast was now covered with writing of all sorts and colors. I had been the first to sign it, right on the top, where he'd see it all the time.

I'd drawn a picture of an owl and a little note to go with it:

Hoo is awesome? You, that's hoo!
Hoo hoo
Your best NOT-friend.
DYNAH!

Oren had laughed and laughed when I was done. But my parents, Nate and Oren's uncle had all looked confused. Which meant it was perfect.

Like he was reading my mind now, Oren said, "I can't wait to get this thing off, but maybe they will let me keep it."

"It kind of stinks," I said, wrinkling my nose. "Take a picture of it." But I was happy he'd want to keep it. I turned my stick to toast the other side of the marshmallow.

"So..." Oren said a few minutes later.

The fire crackled as the grown-ups talked on the other side of the campsite, but he was suddenly really still and quiet.

"What?" I turned toward him for a second, not wanting to take my eye off my marshmallow for too long. They catch fire easily if you aren't careful.

Finally he said, "I went to my first therapy session."

"Oh?" I turned back toward him. "How did it go?"

"It was okay." He shrugged. "Just talking, I guess."

I wanted to ask what he'd talked about, but I didn't. It was to help him with his grief, so he'd probably talked about his parents and the accident. Maybe he'd talked about me and how I'd helped him and we'd become best friends and were going to be in the same class at school— something we were both excited about.

Or maybe he'd mentioned how Nate had taken him to the comic-book store last week, like a big brother would.

Maybe he'd told the therapist how he and his uncle were getting to know each other. Or how while things were still weird with his old friends, they were getting better.

Or perhaps he'd told his therapist about taking over Nate's job at the funeral home, standing across from me and giving out kippahs and offering condolences while I handed out tissues. How it made him feel better to help others.

"Actually..." Oren said softly, his voice trailing off.

I glanced at him. "Actually what?"

"It was better than just okay," he said, letting out a big breath. "It was...I feel...I don't know. It was *good*. I wasn't expecting it to be. But it was."

So yeah. Whatever it was he'd talked about in therapy, it would help him get better. He already *was* better.

"You know," he said. "Someday, if you wanted to come with me...to talk about Sam..."

I pulled my marshmallow out right before it caught on fire. Perfect.

"Evie?"

I had to swallow past the lump in my throat before I could talk. It wasn't there so much because I was sad about Sam, but because Oren got it. He got *me*.

"Maybe someday," I said, nodding at him. "I'll think on it, okay?"

"Okay." He gave me a smile.

It was then that I realized, too late, I should have gotten my graham crackers ready. Now I'd have to fumble while the marshmallow got cold and lost its gooeyness.

But then Oren was there, holding crackers out to me, chocolate already in place. "Here," he said. "I got you."

I knew he meant more than just the s'mores. No matter what happened, he'd always have my back, same as I'd have his.

Smiling at him, I said, "We make a great team, Zombie Boy."

He grinned and nodded his head, leaning into my shoulder. "Yeah, we sure do, Corpse Girl."

Acknowledgments

Well. Here I am again—in the enviable place of thanking all the people who helped make my book what it is. I am so, so grateful to have this book out in the world, but it's bittersweet because part of what shaped it is, as you can probably imagine, personal loss and my own experience with grief.

When I first had the idea, it was supposed to be a companion novel to my debut, *Small Medium at Large*, a book about a girl who gets hit by lightning and can suddenly hear ghosts. The plan was for this book to be about a boy who would also encounter mostly friendly and meddlesome ghosts, thanks to spending time at his family's funeral home business. I'd even done some preliminary research, touring the Jewish funeral chapel my father manages.

But then I lost my mom. And a weird and very unexpected thing happened. When we went to the funeral home to make all the arrangements, I felt comforted by what I knew, having had special behind-the-scenes access. I'd already seen the inner workings, thanks to my research, and knew what would happen to my mom between the time of her death and the time of her burial. And while I wasn't okay with losing her at all, I felt better for knowing how she would be cared for and the details of the rituals that would be performed to honor her. It struck me that not everyone has that prior knowledge, especially kids.

So that's where this book really came from. And that's why it's dedicated to my dad, the man who works tirelessly to look after the families he takes "into his care," as he often puts it. Dad, your work is important, necessary and appreciated. You do it with a sense of duty, respect and honor, and I think I can speak for everyone when I say that you go above and beyond in every way to make people as comfortable as possible in their most difficult times. You are a true mensch.

I hope my mom is watching and knows that this book would not exist without her too. I mean, I would rather have you here with us, Mom, but I think you'll appreciate the hand you had in making this book what it turned out to be. I know you would have liked it, and don't worry, I know you and dad are both very proud. I also know you are busy hawking this book wherever you are. I can almost hear the pitch amid the click-clack of the mah-jongg tiles: "Four crack, two bam—have I told you about my daughter's latest book?"

But while the origin of this story is very personal and has its roots in my family, making a book requires a lot of people. I have never worked harder on a project to get it just right, so please bear with me.

This incarnation started at the Yiddish Book Center at the Tent: Creative Writing conference I attended back in 2018. Huge thanks to fellow attendees and awesome authors in their own right who read and critiqued the opening pages: Danielle Joseph, Barbara Bietz, Yael Mermelstein, Elie Lichtschein, Evelyn Krieger and Brianna Sayres. Also, thank you to our workshop leader, Kendra Levin, whose words of encouragement and critique were exactly what I needed to carve up the initial pages and get on the right track.

A big thank-you to the amazing people at PJ Library and PJ Our Way, who sponsored Tent and provided a wonderful experience for us all—what an honor to be included. Thank you to Harold Grinspoon and Diane Troderman for making it possible and for opening your home to us for an experience I will truly never forget.

Once the book was drafted, many people read this book along the way: Danielle Joseph and Barbara Bietz (both who read again!), Terry Lynn Johnson, Helaine Becker, Natalie Hyde and Lisa McMann. Your feedback and cheerleading were invaluable and very much appreciated.

For the finer details, thank you again to my dad, Dan Levy. Not only were you my inspiration, but you were also my funeral expert, one willing to read multiple drafts. I did try to be as accurate as possible with the details in this book, but any persisting errors are my own.

Thank you to Rabbi Yonah Lavery-Yisraeli for assisting me with advice about sacred texts.

The Ontario Arts Council gets big kudos for its financial support of this project through Recommender Grants. Many authors would not be able to make their works without its generous support. Thank you to the OAC for recognizing the value of art and artists.

And now for my publishing family—and yes, after this many books, it does feel like a family. A big thank-you to Andrew Wooldridge for heading up the team and sticking it out through even the most challenging times. Hopefully by the time this book is out, 2020 is a very distant memory.

To Olivia, who isn't just a hardworking marketing partner but also came up with the amazing and perfect title for this book. Nailed it!

To the rest of the Orca family pod: Ruth, Kennedy, Susan, Leslie, Ella, Mark, Vivian, Terri and everyone else who had a hand in making this book, I'm toasting you around the virtual dinner table.

A big thank you to Rachel Page, who worked tirelessly to get this cover just right. Creating cover art to represent a tween book about funerals must have been a daunting task, but you nailed it.

And to my editor, Tanya, the best sister-editor an author could ask for. My warmest and most heartfelt thanks for championing this book and me again. You aren't just a great editor but a very fine human being who gets me 99.9 percent of the time, which leaves very little room for meanness.

Thank you to my agent, Hilary McMahon, for your comments, advice, helpful suggestions and tireless support of me and my books. Here's to many more.

And, as always, I have to thank my actual family. Besides my dad, there is always and forever my husband, Deke. It feels both redundant and absolutely appropriate and necessary to thank you for being the best partner in all of this. You are my rock and most steadfast supporter, and that never goes unnoticed. Thank you for the plot assistance, for listening and for just being there to cheer me on. You are the very best.

No thanks to my pets for anything to do with this book. None of you deserve it. I'm just kidding! Treats for everyone!

Joanne Levy is the author of a number of books for young people, including *Double Trouble* and *Fish Out of Water* in the Orca Currents line and the middle-grade novels *The Sun Will Come Out* and *Small Medium At Large*, which was nominated for the Red Maple Award. She lives in Clinton, Ontario.